Love at the Ritz

The Marquis said in a rather strange voice:

"I love you! You know I love you more than I have ever loved any woman in my whole life! But I cannot marry you!"

Vilma could not speak.

She could only stare at him, thinking that what she was hearing could not be true.

The Marquis put out his hand to take hers before he said:

"I will arrange somehow to have you near me, whether we are in London or in the country."

Slowly Vilma began to understand what he was asking of her.

She felt as if the floor had opened beneath her feet to reveal a dark chasm into which she was falling . . .

A Camfield Novel of Love by Barbara Cartland

"Barbara Cartland's novels are distinguished by their intelligence, good sense, and good nature. . . ."

—ROMANTIC TIMES

"Who could give better advice on how to keep your romance going strong than the world's most famous romance novelist, Barbara Cartland?"

—THE STAR

Camfield Place,
Hatfield
Hertfordshire,
England

Dearest Reader,

Camfield Novels of Love mark a very exciting era of my books with Jove. They have already published nearly two hundred of my titles since they became my first publisher in America, and now all my original paperback romances in the future will be published exclusively by them.

As you already know, Camfield Place in Hertfordshire is my home, which originally existed in 1275, but was rebuilt in 1867 by the grandfather of Beatrix Potter.

It was here in this lovely house, with the best view in the county, that she wrote *The Tale of Peter Rabbit*. Mr. McGregor's garden is exactly as she described it. The door in the wall that the fat little rabbit could not squeeze underneath and the goldfish pool where the white cat sat twitching its tail are still there.

I had Camfield Place blessed when I came here in 1950 and was so happy with my husband until he died, and now with my children and grandchildren, that I know the atmosphere is filled with love and we have all been very lucky.

It is easy here to write of love and I know you will enjoy the Camfield Novels of Love. Their plots are definitely exciting and the covers very romantic. They come to you, like all my books, with love.

Bless you,

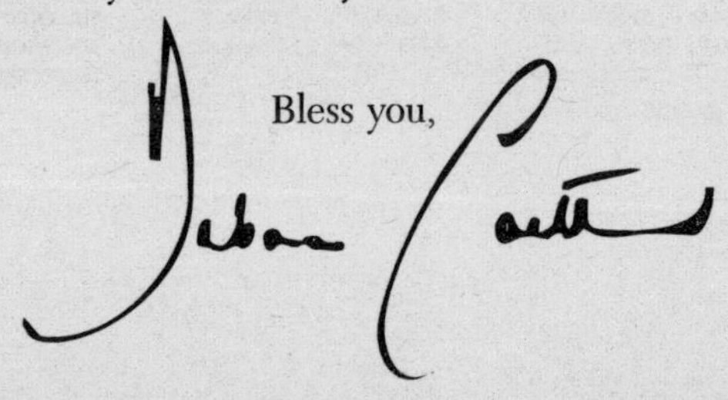

CAMFIELD NOVELS OF LOVE

by Barbara Cartland

THE POOR GOVERNESS
WINGED VICTORY
LUCKY IN LOVE
LOVE AND THE MARQUIS
A MIRACLE IN MUSIC
LIGHT OF THE GODS
BRIDE TO A BRIGAND
LOVE COMES WEST
A WITCH'S SPELL
SECRETS
THE STORMS OF LOVE
MOONLIGHT ON THE SPHINX
WHITE LILAC
REVENGE OF THE HEART
THE ISLAND OF LOVE
THERESA AND A TIGER
LOVE IS HEAVEN
MIRACLE FOR A MADONNA
A VERY UNUSUAL WIFE
THE PERIL AND THE PRINCE
ALONE AND AFRAID
TEMPTATION OF A TEACHER
ROYAL PUNISHMENT
THE DEVILISH DECEPTION
PARADISE FOUND
LOVE IS A GAMBLE
A VICTORY FOR LOVE
LOOK WITH LOVE
NEVER FORGET LOVE
HELGA IN HIDING
SAFE AT LAST
HAUNTED
CROWNED WITH LOVE
ESCAPE
THE DEVIL DEFEATED
THE SECRET OF THE MOSQUE
A DREAM IN SPAIN
THE LOVE TRAP
LISTEN TO LOVE
THE GOLDEN CAGE
LOVE CASTS OUT FEAR
A WORLD OF LOVE
DANCING ON A RAINBOW
LOVE JOINS THE CLANS
AN ANGEL RUNS AWAY
FORCED TO MARRY
BEWILDERED IN BERLIN
WANTED—A WEDDING RING
THE EARL ESCAPES
STARLIGHT OVER TUNIS
THE LOVE PUZZLE
LOVE AND KISSES
SAPPHIRES IN SIAM
A CARETAKER OF LOVE
SECRETS OF THE HEART
RIDING IN THE SKY
LOVERS IN LISBON
LOVE IS INVINCIBLE
THE GODDESS OF LOVE
AN ADVENTURE OF LOVE
THE HERB FOR HAPPINESS
ONLY A DREAM
SAVED BY LOVE
LITTLE TONGUES OF FIRE
A CHIEFTAIN FINDS LOVE
A LOVELY LIAR
THE PERFUME OF THE GODS
A KNIGHT IN PARIS
REVENGE IS SWEET
THE PASSIONATE PRINCESS
SOLITA AND THE SPIES
THE PERFECT PEARL
LOVE IS A MAZE
A CIRCUS FOR LOVE
THE TEMPLE OF LOVE
THE BARGAIN BRIDE
THE HAUNTED HEART
REAL LOVE OR FAKE
KISS FROM A STRANGER
A VERY SPECIAL LOVE
THE NECKLACE OF LOVE
A REVOLUTION OF LOVE
THE MARQUIS WINS
LOVE IS THE KEY
LOVE AT FIRST SIGHT
THE TAMING OF A TIGRESS
PARADISE IN PENANG
THE EARL RINGS A BELLE
THE QUEEN SAVES THE KING
NO DISGUISE FOR LOVE
LOVE LIFTS THE CURSE
BEAUTY OR BRAINS?
TOO PRECIOUS TO LOSE
HIDING
A TANGLED WEB
JUST FATE
A MIRACLE IN MEXICO
WARNED BY A GHOST
TWO HEARTS IN HUNGARY
A THEATER OF LOVE
A DYNASTY OF LOVE
MAGIC FROM THE HEART
THE WINDMILL OF LOVE
LOVE STRIKES A DEVIL
LOVE AND WAR
SEEK THE STARS
A CORONATION OF LOVE
A WISH COME TRUE
LOVED FOR HIMSELF
A KISS IN ROME
HIDDEN BY LOVE
BORN OF LOVE
WALKING TO WONDERLAND
TERROR FROM THE THRONE
THE CAVE OF LOVE
THE PEAKS OF ECSTASY
LUCKY LOGAN FINDS LOVE
THE ANGEL AND THE RAKE
THE QUEEN OF HEARTS
THE WICKED WIDOW
TO SCOTLAND AND LOVE

A NEW CAMFIELD NOVEL OF LOVE BY

BARBARA CARTLAND

Love at the Ritz

JOVE BOOKS, NEW YORK

LOVE AT THE RITZ

A Jove Book / published by arrangement with
the author

PRINTING HISTORY
Jove edition / October 1993

ISBN: 0-515-11219-4

A JOVE BOOK®
Jove Books are published by The Berkley Publishing Group,
200 Madison Avenue, New York, New York 10016.
JOVE and the "J" design are trademarks belonging to Jove Publications, Inc.

PRINTED IN THE UNITED STATES OF AMERICA

10 9 8 7 6 5 4 3 2 1

Dedication

THIS book is dedicated to the most famous, most comfortable, and the most glamorous Hotel in the world.

I spent my Honeymoon at The Ritz, and I went back every year—except during the War—for a Second Honeymoon with my husband, who died after 28 blissful years of marriage, of his War wounds contracted at Passchendaele.

The Ritz has a magic for me that no other Hotel has and this book is therefore a tribute to the wonders created with love by César Ritz.

Author's Note

I HAVE been visiting The Ritz for sixty-six years, and it is without exception the most comfortable and, I think, the most attractive Hotel in the world.

It always delights me to think it is really unchanged since it was designed by César Ritz and opened in June 1898.

César Ritz was, in fact, a genius and far in advance of his time. Nobody had ever envisaged a Hotel with a bathroom to every bedroom, and one which was decorated in such perfect taste.

When I lie in bed in The Ritz now, looking at the plain walls which were a great innovation in César Ritz's day, the fine silk curtains with no frills or furbelows, and the beautiful chandelier which is part of the story I have just written, I think how lucky we were that César Ritz created a revolution in the Hotel business.

He had an obsession with cleanliness, which again

was new, and he was later to make the Carlton Hotel in London, which now has been demolished, a replica of The Ritz in Paris.

The Ritz has a history of its own, from the time The Prince of Wales became its most important customer to when the Germans took it over as their Headquarters when they reached Paris in World War II.

I have spent some of the happiest days of my life in The Ritz, as I went there on my Honeymoon. Every year, except during the War, my husband and I went back for a Second Honeymoon to revive our romance and to keep our love even more entrancing than it had been when we first married.

If we ever lost The Ritz it would not be only a loss to France, but to all the people like myself who have enjoyed it generation after generation.

Love at the Ritz

chapter one

1898

THE Earl of Cuttesdale was in an exceedingly bad temper.

He had been in a rage when he left London because his back was hurting him so much that it was an agony to move.

At least, he told himself, he would try something new.

At the same time, he continued to abuse the English Medical Profession all the way across the Channel and again on the train journey to Paris.

His daughter Vilma, who was with him, was used to his rages and, therefore, paid little attention.

His valet, Herbert, who had been with him for years, had learnt to say nothing until the storm was over.

When they'd neared Paris, the Earl had said to them both:

"Now you quite understand, as I have no wish for anyone to know that I am like a broken doll, I am from this moment Colonel Crawshaw and Lady Vilma is Miss Crawshaw."

As he had already stressed this at least a dozen times, Vilma thought that neither she nor Herbert were likely to forget it.

They drove to Paris to the luxurious house which the Earl had borrowed on previous occasions from his friend the *Vicomte* de Servaiss.

The *Vicomte,* at the moment, was in the country.

He had, however, replied to the Earl's letter saying he was only too delighted for him to use his house in the *Rue St. Honoré.*

Vilma had never been there before.

She was delighted with the beauty of the rooms and the way they were lit in the new fashion by electricity.

"It is very pleasing, Papa," she said, "to see that the way we have done it at home is absolutely correct, for I believe that the French are more advanced in electrical matters than we are."

The Earl merely glowered in reply.

He was assisted up to bed so that he could rest his back.

In the morning he was slightly better-tempered when Vilma brought him the newspapers.

"It is so thrilling, Papa," she said. "The new Hotel Ritz was opened yesterday and apparently all the important people we have ever heard of were there."

"I dislike Hotels!" the Earl said firmly.

"I know, Papa, but they say the Ritz is quite different from any other Hotel that has ever been. Can you imagine that there is a bathroom for every bedroom?"

For a moment the Earl looked as if he admitted that this was a good innovation.

Then he said:

"The Prince of Wales is perfectly content to stay at the Bristol, where there is only one bathroom on each floor."

Vilma was not listening. She was reading the newspaper.

She could read French as easily as she could read English.

After a long pause, she said:

"Fancy! The Vanderbilts were at the opening, and so were the Grand Dukes Michael and Alexander, and the beautiful Otero. I am sure I have heard of her before."

"If you have, you should not have!" the Earl snapped.

"Why not?" Vilma asked.

The Earl paused for a moment for words.

Then he said:

"She is a Courtesan, I admit a grand one, but nevertheless her name would never have been mentioned by your Mother or by your Grandmother."

Vilma laughed.

"You know, Papa, that you and I can talk about everything, and that is what I enjoy more than anything else."

The Earl's eyes softened.

He was, in fact, very fond of his daughter.

He thought her so beautiful that it was unlikely, now she was launched in Society, that he would keep her for long.

He had, however, by taking her away in June, made

her miss some of the most important Balls that were taking place in London.

However, she did not seem to mind.

In fact, she was far more interested in going to Paris than in attending the elaborate functions given by the Mothers of her contemporaries.

Reading the newspaper again she exclaimed:

"The English were there too—the Duke of Marlborough, the Dukes of Portland, Sutherland, and Norfolk—all there with their wives."

"That is something new!" the Earl exclaimed. "In my day, when one came to Paris, one left one's wife behind."

Vilma laughed.

"Now, that, Papa, is just the sort of thing you ought not to say to me!"

"You brought it on yourself," the Earl retorted. "Now, make sure that none of that lot learn that I am here. I have no wish for them to laugh and jeer at me because, for the first time in years, I have fallen off a horse."

"It is understandable, Papa," Vilma said, "considering how wild *Hercules* is. But you would ride him."

The Earl knew this was true.

He was a magnificent rider.

He was quite confident that the stallion he had bought from a friend because he could not control it would be "child's play" as far as he was concerned.

Unfortunately, *Hercules*, who was a very fine stallion, had shied at one of the spotted deer in the Park.

The Earl, taken unawares, had been thrown heavily.

Vilma knew only too well how proud her Father was of his Equestrian reputation.

She knew he would feel very hurt if any of his friends crowed over him because he was *hors de combat*.

"No one will know you are here, Papa," she said soothingly, "and I will be very careful to remember that I am Miss Crawshaw. After all, I shall not be lying, as it is one of your names."

The Earl belonged to a very old family going back to pre-Tudor times.

"Crawshaw" was one of the titles his forebears had collected over the centuries.

He regularly used it when he went abroad, especially when he did not wish to be made a fuss of by the British Embassy, or pursued by title-seeking foreigners.

But he had never been more eager to be incognito than he was at this moment.

He thought with a little shudder how Marlborough, who had a somewhat spiteful sense of humour, would make the most of his humiliating condition.

Because he was looking depressed, Vilma went up to his bed and, bending down, kissed his cheek.

"Cheer up, Papa!" she urged. "I am sure this man will work miracles on you and you will soon be back, riding as you always do, to the delight and envy of everyone who sees you."

"You are a good girl, Vilma," the Earl said, "and I will break in that damned stallion if it kills me."

Vilma knew it was no use arguing.

She therefore continued reading about the opening of the Ritz Hotel.

The newspapers reported how amazed everybody was at what they found there.

Because César Ritz had caused a sensation, the newspapers all carried many columns concerning his career.

They described how he had been determined to build a Hotel that was different from all others.

Reading on, she learned that César Ritz had been born in the Swiss village of Niederwald in 1850.

He was the thirteenth child of a peasant couple whose family line was long, if humble.

The stone-stove in their living-room bore a crest which had been reproduced on the Hotel writing-paper.

César had looked after goats and cows belonging to his Father, who was Mayor of the village.

It had a population of about two-hundred.

The boy went to a local School, although his Father was of the opinion that it was a waste of time.

His Mother, however, was ambitious for her children.

César, when he was very young, knew exactly what he wished to do.

When he was twelve, he was sent to Sion to learn French and Mathematics.

He was impatient to get on, and became an apprentice wine-waiter.

When she read this, Vilma looked up at her Father and said:

"This is a fascinating account of César Ritz's life in *Le Jour*, Papa. I know you would like to read it."

"I am not interested in waiters," the Earl replied.

"He is much more important than that now," Vilma replied, "though he did spend some time polishing floors, scrubbing, and running up and down stairs with luggage and trays."

"I cannot think why you do not read something intelligent," the Earl said as if he wanted to find fault. "Here we are in Paris, which is the most civilised City in the world, and you spend your time drooling over some obscure Hotel Proprietor."

Vilma laughed.

She knew that her Father always took the opposite view to herself, which was one of the things which made their conversations sparkle.

They were always antagonists, straining their brains to the utmost capacity to defeat each other in argument.

"Well, all I can say," she said, "is that I would love to visit the Ritz Hotel and see how different it is from anywhere else we have stayed. Imagine it, Papa! No heavy tapestries, plushes, or velvet because *Monsieur* Ritz says 'they collect the dust.' "

"I should think the place looks like an Army Barracks!" the Earl growled.

His daughter did not answer; she was reading on.

Then she exclaimed:

"What do you think it says here?"

There was no reply, but she continued:

"The comfortable dining-room chairs were only delivered the day before yesterday, and when they were, *Monsieur* Ritz found that the tables were too high.

" 'They must go back to be cut down,' he cried.

"His wife agreed and he ran outside to see the van that had delivered the chairs moving away. He ran after it in the rain and shouted:

" 'Two centimetres off every table-leg and they must be back in two hours!'

"He was told it was impossible, but he got his own way and the tables came back. The waiters were finishing laying them as the first of the guests' carriages arrived."

"He should not have left it to the eleventh hour," the Earl remarked.

"I think it is a fascinating story," Vilma asserted. "Please, please, Papa, before we leave Paris, take me to see the Ritz Hotel."

"And meet someone I know there?" the Earl asked. "Certainly not! As soon as I am better, we will go back to London and you shall dance at what Balls are left."

Vilma did not reply.

She was thinking that she must see a little of Paris before they returned to London.

She had already made a list of the places she wanted to visit.

It started with the Louvre and ended with the Aquarium in the *Bois*.

The difficulty, of course, would be to find someone to accompany her.

She knew she could not go out alone.

Because her Father was so determined that no-one should gossip about his injuries, she had not been allowed to bring her lady's-maid with her.

She knew it would be impossible to get Herbert to leave his master.

"I will think of something," she told herself rather doubtfully, and went on reading about the Ritz.

* * *

Later in the day the man who everybody had said was so successful with injured backs arrived.

His name was Pierre Blanc.

Vilma saw him first, to explain what had happened.

She spoke to him in her fluent French.

She made him understand how important it was that her Father should be able to ride again as soon as possible.

"He is a famous rider in England," she said, "and that is why he does not want anyone to know what has happened to him."

"I can understand that, *Mademoiselle,*" the man said, "and I promise that *Monsieur* will soon be well again and will find it difficult to remember that he was ever frustrated in such an unfortunate manner."

He spoke so confidently that Vilma was delighted.

"I hope you will make my Father feel that it will be only a short time before he is well. He very much dislikes being an invalid."

Pierre Blanc spread out his hands.

"What man does not?" he asked. "Especially when he is in Paris."

"Now I will take you upstairs," Vilma said.

"But before we do so, *Mademoiselle,*" Pierre Blanc interrupted, "you must promise me you will make your Father follow my instructions to the letter."

"I will try," Vilma answered a little doubtfully.

"The most important thing is for him to rest after I have given him each treatment," Pierre Blanc said. "In nearly every case the patient goes straight to sleep. But if your Father does not, he is to lie quietly on his back undisturbed and not agitated by anything or anyone. Do you understand, *Mademoiselle*?"

"Of course I do, *Monsieur,*" Vilma replied, "and I promise you that Papa will be left very quiet, with nobody and nothing to disturb him."

"That is exactly what is required," Pierre Blanc exclaimed. "And now, *Mademoiselle,* I am ready to meet my patient."

Vilma took him upstairs to the comfortable room which her Father was using.

It was the largest in the house.

She knew, although her Father would never admit it, that he had been counting the hours until Pierre Blanc arrived.

As the two men shook hands, Vilma slipped downstairs.

Now she was free, and perhaps she could go somewhere and see a little, if only a very little, of Paris.

She wondered whether she could ask one of the maid-servants to go with her.

But she had noticed that they were all middle-aged or old.

She thought they might resent being asked to accompany her in the afternoon, when they had been working all the morning.

"I must go out—I must!" she said to herself.

To her surprise, the door opened.

A man-servant with grey hair, who she had already learnt had been with the *Vicomte* for thirty years, said:

"Monsieur César Ritz to see you, *M'mselle."*

Vilma was so surprised that she thought for a moment that it must be a joke.

Then a short, dark man came into the room.

She knew from the illustrations she had seen in the newspapers that it was indeed César Ritz who stood there.

There was no mistaking the high forehead, from which the hair grew far back, and the drooping moustache.

It was the Hotelier in person.

She could only stare at him as he crossed the room to bow respectfully and say:

"Forgive me, *Mademoiselle,* for disturbing you, but I have a great favour to ask. It is only just now that I have learnt that the house is not empty, as I had expected, but that you and your Father are staying here."

"We arrived the day before yesterday," Vilma explained.

"That is what the servant told me," César Ritz replied, "and I must therefore explain to you why I am here."

He looked worried as he spoke, as if he feared she might refuse to grant him the request he was going to make.

"Suppose you sit down, *Monsieur* Ritz," Vilma said. "I have just been reading about your magnificent Hotel."

As she spoke, she indicated the nearest armchair, and as he sat down, César Ritz said:

"I was fortunate, very fortunate. As you can imagine, *Mademoiselle,* there was always the fear at the back of my mind that those on whom I counted would not come. But they did! Almost every one of them. But in doing so, they have created for me a problem."

"A problem?" Vilma asked.

"That is the reason why I am here," César Ritz replied.

"Tell me what it is," Vilma prompted him.

César Ritz drew in his breath before he said:

"I never dreamt, I was never presumptuous enough to imagine that every room would be booked so soon. But, believe it or not, *Mademoiselle*, the Hotel is already full!"

Vilma thought he sounded like an excited School-Boy, and she smiled as she replied:

"I am so glad, *Monsieur*. It must be a great satisfaction for you, after working so hard, to know that you are really appreciated."

"I am indeed very grateful," César Ritz said. "But there is one deficiency, and I swore to myself that when I opened the Ritz it would be as perfect as it was possible for any Hotel to be."

"That is what I have been reading in the newspapers," Vilma said, "and I am sure it is perfect."

"There is, unfortunately, one flaw," César Ritz replied.

"What can that be?" Vilma asked.

"For the chandeliers in the bedrooms, I used as a model one in this house. It was in fact the *Vicomte* de Servaiss who told me he considered it one of the most attractive designs he had ever seen."

"So you had it copied," Vilma said.

"Exactly!" César Ritz replied. "But while they were being installed, one got broken."

"How tiresome!" Vilma exclaimed.

"Yes, indeed," César Ritz agreed, "but it would not have mattered so much if the room did not have to be occupied to-night by the *Comte* Gaston de Forêt, a very important person in Paris."

He paused and then continued:

"There is nowhere else I can put him—nowhere! And there is no chandelier in his bedroom."

He made it sound such a disaster that it was with difficulty that Vilma did not laugh.

"Then how can we help you, *Monsieur*?" she enquired.

"I knew when I came here," *Monsieur* Ritz replied, "that the *Vicomte,* whom I have served for years and who has encouraged me in my ambitions, would have lent me one of the chandeliers from this house until the replacement that is being made for me is delivered."

His voice dropped as he pleaded:

"Please, *Mademoiselle,* please, be generous and allow me to have one, just for the few days which must elapse before the replacement I have ordered comes from the factory."

Vilma smiled.

"But, of course, *Monsieur,* it will be a pleasure. I am certain there are quite a number in the house, and you can choose the one you want."

César Ritz clasped his hands together.

"Merci, merci, Mademoiselle, you are more than kind! I cannot express my gratitude! How could I place the *Comte* in a room that is incomplete and with no light in the centre of its ceiling?"

Vilma rose.

"Come and see which one you require," she said.

She walked towards the door, and César Ritz opened it for her.

As the chandelier he required was for a bedroom, she knew that those in the Reception Rooms would be too large.

She went up the stairs and opened the door of a bedroom that was not in use.

Hanging from the ceiling was an elegant chandelier which was a duplicate of the one in her room.

It was a bowl-like shape with six candles suspended from it.

Looking at the ceiling, César Ritz clasped his hands together.

"That is exactly what I require, exactly what I have ordered," he said, "except that it is not fitted for electricity. But it is quite easy to adapt it, and I am sure *Monsieur le Vicomte* will be delighted when I return it to him if it can be electrically lit, as most are in the house."

"I thought how skilfully some of the chandeliers have already been adapted," Vilma said. "At the same time, the *Vicomte* also uses candles, which I think are more becoming."

"You have not seen my lighting," César Ritz replied. "I spent hours, literally hours, *Mademoiselle,* choosing what I thought was the most attractive colour, especially for beautiful women."

"I read about that," Vilma murmured.

"Day after day," *Monsieur* Ritz explained, "I worked with the Electrician, trying out the effects of various colours on my wife's complexion."

He made a gesture with his hands before he went on:

"I finally decided that a delicate shade of apricot pink was the most becoming to her, and that is what I have used throughout the Hotel."

"It sounds wonderful!" Vilma exclaimed. "I do wish I could see it!"

"Why not?" César Ritz replied. "I would be very

proud to show you, *Mademoiselle,* what I have achieved in making my dream become reality."

He saw the expression in Vilma's eyes and said:

"Come with me, *Mademoiselle,* come with me now! I know you will not be surprised to learn that I have an Electrician outside who will remove this chandelier so that we can take it with us."

Vilma drew in her breath.

She knew it was something she should not do.

But her Father must remain quiet after his treatment, so he would not know that she had left the house.

For a moment she hesitated.

Then, because the temptation was too great, she said:

"Call your Electrician, *Monsieur,* and I will put on my hat so that I can accompany you."

"You are very gracious," César Ritz answered.

He hurried down the stairs, moving more like a young boy than a man of his age.

The Electrician was surprisingly quick in taking down the chandelier.

By the time Vilma came from her bedroom, César Ritz was waiting for her in the Hall.

Outside was a very comfortable carriage, drawn by two horses.

The Electrician climbed up on the box beside the coachman, while Vilma and César Ritz sat inside.

Only as they turned into the *Place Vendôme* did she manage to say:

"I think you will understand, *Monsieur,* when I say that it would be a mistake for me to meet anyone from London. My Father has no wish for his friends to know he is in Paris. He had a slight accident and is here for special treatment."

To emphasise what she had already said, she added:

"He is allowed no visitors, and it would be very embarrassing for me to have to turn people away."

"Yes, of course, *Mademoiselle,* I understand," César Ritz replied. "We will not drive in to the grand entrance, here in the *Place Vendôme,* but will enter by the back of the Hotel—which was my intention anyway."

Vilma knew this was because he did not want anyone to know that he had been forced to borrow a chandelier for his "perfect" Hotel.

When she stepped out of the carriage César Ritz hurried her up a side staircase which led to the First Floor.

"I want you to see one of the best suites in the Hotel," he said, "which fortunately will not be occupied until this evening. The guests who were in it yesterday left this morning."

Vilma was already appreciating that the passages were lofty and painted rather than covered with wallpaper.

The attractive carpet was bright but traditional in design.

César Ritz showed her into a large Suite overlooking the *Place Vendôme.*

Vilma was entranced by the luxury of it.

The walls were bare except for large mirrors.

There were, as she had read in the newspapers, no plushes or velvet, nor were there any frills or "furbelows" to the curtains.

"I will not have wooden beds," César Ritz explained in the bedroom. "Brass is more hygienic."

As Vilma expected, the lighting was an apricot pink.

She knew at night it would make any woman look her best.

There were built-in cupboards, and the Sitting-Room was furnished with large, comfortable armchairs.

There were flowers and bowls of exotic fruit waiting for the incoming guests.

"It is lovely, *Monsieur*, absolutely lovely!" Vilma exclaimed.

They walked a long way down the passage until they came to the room that had no chandelier.

In the other rooms they were suspended from the ceilings by silken cords.

Now in the room they entered the cords were there, but no chandelier.

"I quite see why you so desperately needed the chandelier you have just borrowed from the *Vicomte*," Vilma remarked.

"All thanks to you, *Mademoiselle*," César Ritz said gallantly. "If you had refused me, I think I should have sat down on your doorstep and cried!"

Vilma laughed.

"We could not allow you to do that, not when you are the King of all the Hotels and the most acclaimed man in Paris."

She saw how delighted César Ritz was by the compliment.

It sounded even better, she thought, when it was spoken in French rather than in English.

It was then, as they were talking, that the Electrician came in with a folding ladder.

He set it up in the centre of the room.

Following him came two servants carrying the chandelier.

They held it up so that the Electrician fastened it to the silken cords.

Vilma had watched the Electricians at home when they were wiring her Father's chandeliers.

She thought this man was more skilful at his job than the Englishman had been.

She was still watching when somebody came into the room to whisper in César Ritz's ear.

"Forgive me, *Mademoiselle,*" he said, "if I leave you, but I am needed elsewhere. I will be back as soon as I possibly can."

"Of course, *Monsieur,*" Vilma agreed. "I will be quite happy here."

He bowed to her, then hurried away.

Vilma continued to watch the Electrician.

Having finished connecting the wiring to the lamp-holders, he climbed down the ladder and said:

"I have to get the light-bulbs, *M'mselle.*"

When he had gone, Vilma looked up at the chandelier.

She saw that there were several dirty marks on the bowl from the hands of those who had carried it.

She was quite sure they would displease César Ritz when he returned.

What he had said to her, and what she had read, told her he was a fanatic where cleanliness was concerned.

So she decided to remove the marks.

She looked around.

The door to the bathroom was open, and she found a towelling-flannel there, put ready for the expected guest.

She thought the bathroom was very elegant with a profusion of mirrors.

The bath-taps and those on the basin were of gold.

She went back into the bedroom.

She was just about to climb up the ladder, when she realised her hat would get in her way.

Taking it off, she set it down on a chair with her gloves before she climbed up the ladder.

She rubbed the marks gently and was relieved to find they came off easily.

She found also that the chandelier was rather dusty.

She was cleaning the inside of the bowl when a voice below her said:

"What pretty Angel has just come down from Heaven to illuminate me just when I most need it?"

Vilma looked down and saw there was a very smartly-dressed man staring up at her.

He was obviously a Frenchman, and she guessed that he was between thirty and forty.

But the expression in his eyes and the manner in which he spoke made her feel a little nervous.

"I . . . I was just dusting the chandelier, *Monsieur*," she replied.

"As doubtless you polish the stars that gleam in the sky," he answered.

Again, the way he spoke made Vilma feel embarrassed, and she looked away from him and said quickly:

"I . . . I have finished . . . now."

"Then I will help you down to earth," the Frenchman said, moving nearer.

He put up his arms as if to take hold of her, but Vilma said hurriedly:

"No, no . . . I need no help. Just leave me . . . alone."

"That is something, my very lovely angel, I have no intention of doing," the Frenchman said. "You have come from the sky into my room, and why should I refuse a gift from the Gods?"

Vilma knew that he was the *Comte* Gaston de Forêt.

He put out his hand as he spoke, and she felt him touch her ankle.

She knew that if she moved off the ladder, he would take her into his arms.

"Please . . . leave me alone, *Monsieur,*" she said angrily, "you have no . . . right to . . . touch me!"

"Let me explain to you what right I have," the *Comte* replied. "I want, more than I have wanted anything for a long time, to hold you close to me."

The assured way he spoke frightened Vilma.

She knew if she moved one step down he would be able to get his arms round her.

She was terrified that if he did so he would then try to kiss her.

She had never been in such a situation before, and she had no idea what to do next.

"Go away, *Monsieur,*" she said. "I wish to descend from this ladder and . . . leave the . . . room."

"That is something I shall certainly prevent you from doing," the *Comte* replied.

His fingers tightened on her ankle, and she thought he was going to pull her down towards him.

Holding tightly to the top of the ladder, Vilma screamed:

"Help! Help!"

Even as she did so, she knew that it was too soon for either the Electrician or *Monsieur* Ritz to return.

She felt the Frenchman's hand move a little further up her leg and screamed again.

"Help me, somebody! Oh, please . . . help me!"

Because she was so frightened, she spoke instinctively in English.

To her surprise and utter relief, she heard an English voice ask:

"Can it be possible that one of my countrywomen is in trouble?"

A man appeared in the doorway, and the *Comte* turned round.

"Oh, it is you, Lynworth!" he exclaimed. "What are you doing here?"

"Obviously coming to the rescue of a damsel in distress," the newcomer replied. "I suppose, de Forêt, you are up to your tricks again."

"This is my room and you have no right to come into it!" the *Comte* retorted.

He was looking angrily at the newcomer.

Vilma slipped down the ladder and round to the other side of it from where the Frenchman was standing.

Then she ran towards the door, fearing he might stop her from reaching it.

She could not pass through it because the tall, broad-shouldered Englishman was standing there.

He put out his hand and took hers, saying:

"You are quite safe now. Like the White Knight, I have saved you from the Dragon!"

He spoke provocatively, and his eyes were twinkling as he looked at the *Comte.*

"One day I will get even with you, Lynworth," he threatened.

"I doubt it, *Monsieur le Comte,*" the Englishman replied, "but of course I am ready to accept any challenge you wish to offer me."

He turned away as he spoke and, taking Vilma by the arm, drew her down the passage.

Only when they had gone a little way from the *Comte*'s room did Vilma say:

"My hat! I have left my hat behind!"

The Englishman drew a key from his pocket and opened a door on the other side of the corridor.

"Wait in here while I fetch it," he said. "You will be quite safe."

Without demur, Vilma went into the room.

Saying no more, he shut the door behind her and she heard the key turn in the lock.

She found herself in an attractive Sitting-Room not unlike the one adjoining the *Comte*'s bedroom.

She was a little breathless from fear and consternation at what had happened.

She told herself severely that it was her own fault.

She should not have come to the Ritz Hotel in the first place.

It had been a great mistake to allow herself to be left alone, and enable the *Comte* to come into the room and assume that she was one of César Ritz's staff.

'Papa would be furious!' she thought.

She felt extremely grateful to the Englishman who had rescued her.

She heard the key turn again in the lock of the door behind her.

A moment later he came into the Sitting-Room with her hat in his hand.

"Your admirer," he said with laughter in his voice, "wished to keep it as a souvenir, but I managed to take it from him."

"Thank you . . . oh . . . thank . . . you!" Vilma cried. "I am so grateful to you for . . . saving me."

chapter two

THE Marquis of Lynworth had come to Paris on an impulse.

He was a handsome, very attractive man who enjoyed life enormously—when he was not being pressured by his relatives into marriage.

He had had an unfortunate love-affair when he was a young man.

It had made him decide that he would not marry until he needed a son in his old age.

As he was now only just over thirty, "old age" seemed a long way off and he was in no hurry.

But he was an only child.

Therefore, not only his Grandparents and his Mother, but innumerable Aunts, Uncles, and Cousins were all insisting in one way or another that he should be married.

The more they badgered him, the more he decided that he would be bored stiff with any woman if she were with him for long, especially the type of woman they considered suitable to be the Marchioness of Lynworth.

He was an exceedingly good rider, an expert Polo-player, and an acknowledged game-shot.

With his ten thousand acres of land to look after, he had plenty to occupy him, and he enjoyed himself to the full in his own way.

There had been, of course, innumerable women in his life.

They were, however, definitely not the marriageable girls whom he saw, gauche and shy, scattered round the Ball-Rooms.

His *affairs de coeur* were conducted with the utmost propriety and so discreetly that in most cases the gossips, whilst suspecting him, had nothing concrete to criticise.

The difficulty was that one by one the Ladies—who always were married—fell in love with him.

A woman in love is jealous and also very possessive.

Over the years the Marquis had learnt, when a love affair was in his own words "getting out of hand," to disappear.

This was something which was happening at the moment.

Lady Maxwell's affection for him was becoming more and more obvious in public.

He therefore had decided that he must ease himself out of a situation which had become not only uncomfortable, but also noticeable.

He was aware that it would not be easy.

He did not wish, unless it was absolutely necessary, to leave London at the height of the Season.

As a most eligible bachelor, he was in demand by all the most important hostesses.

The Prince of Wales included him in every party that was given at Marlborough House.

"Dammit all!" he complained to himself. "Why should I be driven away when I have no wish to leave England."

On his chest-of-drawers was a *billet-doux* from Lady Maxwell.

He knew exactly what she would say and what she wanted.

He thought it was extremely foolish of her to have sent it to his house by one of her husband's grooms wearing her husband's livery.

Not only did grooms talk, but so inevitably did his own servants.

The gossips in the Servants' Halls were notorious for spreading the news of a love-affair from one house to another.

He had not yet opened Lady Maxwell's note, when another letter was brought upstairs.

This one was from his Mother.

He opened it quickly, wondering what it might contain.

In his mother's delicate but clear hand-writing he read:

Dearest,

I am not very well and I want to see you, if possible, immediately. I know it is a bore for you to come to me at a moment's notice, but if you can manage either today or tomorrow, I should be very grateful.

With all my love, Dearest Son, and it will be a delight to see you,

Your affectionate Mother,
Muriel Lynworth

The Marquis looked at what he read with a worried expression on his face.

His Mother, he knew, was in poor health.

He wondered if the Doctors wanted to operate on her, or perhaps take her into a Hospital.

She would view that with horror.

He put down the note and said to his valet:

"Fetch Mr. Butterworth to me immediately."

This was his Secretary, an admirable man who coped with all the arrangements concerning his private life.

He administered Lyn House in London and kept a wary eye on the Marquis's house at Newmarket, and on his Hunting-Lodge in Leicestershire.

He kept in constant touch with his opposite number, another exceedingly competent organiser who looked after Lyn Hall in Oxfordshire and its huge Estate.

The Marquis was nearly dressed by the time Mr. Butterworth came hurrying into the room.

"You wanted me, My Lord," he asked in a slightly breathless voice.

"Yes, Butterworth," the Marquis replied, "I have had a letter from my Mother, asking me to go to see her. Order my Chaise to be round in an hour's time and cancel all my appointments for today."

Mr. Butterworth looked down at his note-book.

"Your Lordship is having luncheon with the Countess de Gary and dining at Marlborough House this evening."

The Marquis thought for a moment.

Then he said:

"I think I should be back in time for Marlborough House, as it annoys His Royal Highness when his numbers are upset at the last moment."

Mr. Butterworth nodded before he said:

"I will notify the Countess that you are unable to be present, and shall I send Her Ladyship some flowers."

"Yes, of course," the Marquis agreed. "A basket of orchids. She is very partial to them."

He could think of a number of other women who liked orchids, mostly, he thought cynically, because they were the most expensive flowers obtainable.

Mr. Butterworth made a note on his pad before he asked:

"Will that be all, My Lord?"

The Marquis hesitated, then as if as an afterthought, he said:

"Send some orchids to Lady Maxwell also and say I am prevented from calling on her this afternoon as arranged."

"Very good, My Lord."

Mr. Butterworth left the room.

The Marquis took a last look at his reflection in the mirror.

He would have been foolish if he had not realised that he was a handsome, in fact, an outstandingly handsome man.

At the same time, there was at the moment a slight frown on his forehead and a tight look to his lips.

It was because he was thinking of how very demanding Lady Maxwell had been last night.

It was at a Ball given by the Duchess of Devonshire.

They had been to different dinner parties.

When he arrived at Devonshire House, Joan Maxwell had given a cry of delight the moment he entered the Ball-Room and moved immediately towards him.

As every Dowager of any importance was present, the Marquis knew her behaviour would not go unnoticed.

Nor would they have missed the look in her eyes as she clung to his arm.

Later she danced closer to him than was circumspect.

As the Marquis looked into the mirror, he saw Lady Maxwell's note reflected in it.

The pale-blue scented envelope was still lying unopened where he had left it.

For a moment he hesitated.

Then, without picking it up, he went from his bedroom.

He did not say anything to his valet.

When he had gone, Barker, who had had long experience of his Master, grinned to himself as he walked across the room.

'That's 'nother one down th' drain!' he was thinking, 'an' not before time!'

The Marquis would have been somewhat concerned if he had known what an acute interest was taken by the members of his household in his love-affairs.

They appraised each new love and were extremely critical of her.

If they did not consider the lady good enough for their Master, they prayed that he would change direction and look elsewhere.

Lady Maxwell was beautiful, no-one could deny that.

Yet, even before the Marquis was aware of it, the servants at Lyn House in Park Lane knew that she was impulsive, slightly unbalanced, and at times even hysterical.

"She'll do 'im no good, an' that's th' truth!" the Butler had said to Barker, who had agreed.

Now Barker picked up the note and laid it in an inconspicuous place on a table near the window.

"If it's forgotten, so much the better! An' 'Er Ladyship'll find 'is orchids cold comfort as a substitute for 'Is Lordship's presence," he remarked out loud.

The Marquis went into the Breakfast-Room which faced into the garden.

His breakfast was ready and waiting for him.

The Breakfast-Room was a small, exquisitely decorated room.

It had been left exactly as Adam, the great Architect and Decorator of the mid-18th century, had designed it.

Like many other rooms in Lyn House, it was a perfect background for the Marquis himself.

He looked far more like a Regency Buck than a conventional man of the '90's.

He enjoyed a good breakfast, waiting on himself, since he preferred it that way in the early morning.

Silence in the Breakfast-Room gave him the opportunity to think clearly.

He disliked even the most skilful servant fidgeting beside him.

When he had finished his breakfast, the Marquis went to his Study.

As he expected, Mr. Butterworth had placed on his desk a number of bills.

There were also several letters which he had dictated, and a pile of invitations.

The Marquis dealt with these first.

Against those he wished to accept he put a large "Y" and those to be refused an "N."

He signed his letters, reading them carefully before he did so.

Afterwards he initialled those bills which were to be paid immediately.

If there was anything to be queried, he put it on one side until he had discussed it with Butterworth.

It was all very well organised, just as he organised his stables, his race-horses, and his Estate.

His friends often said to him:

"I cannot imagine, Lynworth, how you manage to achieve such perfection in everything you do."

"It is just organisation," the Marquis replied.

Although he said it laughingly, he knew it was the truth.

His correspondence finished with, he rang for Mr. Butterworth.

The Secretary hurried to the room.

"I have signed the cheques for the new buildings being erected at Lyn," the Marquis said. "At the same time, I would like you to make certain that everything is in order before you send them."

"I have already done so, My Lord," Mr. Butterworth replied.

"Good!" the Marquis said. "In that case, I will inspect the buildings when I next go to Lyn."

He walked from the Study as he spoke to find that his Chaise was waiting at the front-door.

The Footman on duty in the Hall handed him his top-hat and driving-gloves.

His Chaise was being drawn by some new horses he had bought less than a month ago from a friend who was in urgent need of ready money.

As a team they were perfectly matched and were, he knew, in the prime of condition.

His friend had almost wept at having to part with them.

He had said when he did so:

"If they have to go, I would rather it was you who had them than anybody else. I will not worry that they are not being looked after."

"I promise you they will be, Edward," the Marquis had replied, "and should your financial situation improve, I promise I will let you have them back."

His friend, who faced enormous debts on his Father's death, had said fervently:

"That is just the sort of thing you would say! Thank you, old boy. I only hope that I can pull myself out of the mess I am in at the moment."

"You know I will always help you if I can," the Marquis answered.

His friend touched his shoulder in gratitude.

Now as the Marquis got into the Chaise and picked up the reins, he thought he was going to enjoy driving his friend's team.

The groom jumped up behind, and they were off.

It took him little over an hour to reach his Mother's house, which was near Walton on the River Thames.

It was near a village called Bray.

It was a lovely house to which she had retired after her husband's death.

She said she had never liked the Dower House on the Lyn Estate.

She also preferred to be nearer London so that her friends could visit her more easily.

The Marquis had found the house for her.

He'd furnished it with all the things she treasured ever since she had married when she was just eighteen.

It had been a happy marriage despite the fact that the Marquis had been much older than she was.

Their only sadness was that they had produced only one child.

They would have liked at least half-a-dozen.

Their son, Vernon, however, more than compensated.

He was an outstanding School-Boy and was also very popular.

Academically he did very well at Oxford.

When he went into the Household Cavalry, there was, his Mother thought, no Officer more efficient.

Queen Victoria, who was known for her predilection for handsome men, certainly had a "soft spot" for the Marquis.

The Courtiers at Windsor Castle used to say amongst themselves that he "got away with murder" where she was concerned, and anybody else would have been in disgrace.

The old servants who had moved from Lyn Hall to be with her were obviously awaiting his arrival.

As the Marquis drove up, the front-door was opened with a flourish.

A footman, who was in his forties, ran a red carpet down the steps.

The old Butler, who was getting on for seventy, stood smartly to attention in the doorway.

"Welcome, M'Lord—welcome!" he said. "It's a sight for sore eyes t' see Your Lordship again!"

"It is nice to see you, Dawlish," the Marquis replied. "How is Her Ladyship?"

"Waiting t' see Your Lordship," Dawlish replied.

The old Butler walked slowly up the stairs as he spoke.

The Marquis had forced himself not to go ahead of him.

Dawlish was a little breathless by the time they reached the landing at the top of the stairs.

The Marquis waited to allow him to reach his Mother's door first.

He knew the servants would be upset if everything was not done formally and properly.

Dawlish knocked on the door.

The lady's-maid, who had obviously been waiting for the sound, opened it.

"His Lordship t' see Her Ladyship," Dawlish announced.

The maid opened the door wider, dropping a curtsy as the Marquis walked in.

It was a beautiful room with a large canopied bed.

The Dowager Marchioness was lying back against lace-edged pillows.

Her white hair was elegantly arranged.

Her face still bore evidence of the beauty which had made her outstanding amongst the Ladies-of-the-Bedchamber to Her Majesty.

"Vernon!" she exclaimed, holding out her hands in welcome. "I have been longing to see you!"

"I came, Mama, as soon as I got your note," the Marquis replied.

He bent down and kissed her on both cheeks.

Then he sat on the side of the bed, holding her hands in his.

The maid had left the room, closing the door behind her, and they were alone.

"Tell me what has upset you, Mama?" the Marquis asked.

"I am afraid, Dearest, it is not very good news from the Doctors."

The Marquis's fingers tightened on hers.

"What is wrong?" he asked.

He knew that his Mother was in delicate health and had been so for the last two years.

The Doctors, however, had assured him there was nothing particular to worry about.

There was no reason to suppose she would not live for a number of years yet.

"I am afraid it is my heart," the Marchioness said now, "and because Sir William has given strict instructions as to what I can do and cannot do, I felt I must tell you."

"Of course I must know," the Marquis said. "And, Mama, you must do exactly as he says."

He bent his head and kissed her hands.

"You know I cannot do without you in my life, and therefore you must take great care of yourself, if only for my sake."

The Marchioness gave a little laugh.

"You know I will do that if you ask me to. And now I want you to do something for me."

"What is that?" the Marquis asked.

He spoke a little warily because he suspected he already knew the answer.

Hesitatingly, the Marchioness said:

"Because, Darling boy . . . I want . . . more than anything in the whole world . . . to hold your son in my arms before I die, I have invited the Princess Helgie of Whitenberg to stay."

The Marquis stared at his Mother as if he could not believe what he had heard.

"Princess Helgie?" he asked. "But why?"

The Marchioness's voice was faint, and there was a long pause before she replied:

"Because, Dearest, I think she will make . . . you an . . . excellent wife."

"But—I am not Royal, and I do not believe for a moment that the Grand Duke would consider me as a son-in-law."

The Marquis spoke harshly.

He was, in fact, astounded by what his mother had said.

Although he suspected she would beg him to find a suitable wife, he had never for a moment imagined that she might actually have arranged it herself.

"The Grand Duke came to see me when he visited England a month ago," the Marchioness said. "I talked to him about Helgie because, if you remember, she is my God-daughter."

She looked up at her son, but he did not say anything and she went on:

"The Grand Duke remarked on how interested in you he had always been, and on your success on the race-course."

Still the Marquis did not speak, and after a moment his Mother said a little faintly:

"I cannot remember now whether it was he who suggested that you and Helgie would make a good match, or whether I did. Anyway, I received a letter from him yesterday to say that he had discussed the matter privately with his Statesmen."

The Marquis moved, but did not speak, and his Mother continued:

"They all agreed there was no reason why the Princess must marry Royalty, since the Grand Duke's third son had created a precedent by marrying a woman from the Spanish aristocracy who was not of Royal Blood."

If his Mother had thrown a bomb at him, the Marquis could not have been more surprised, or, indeed, more horrified.

He knew the Grand Duke Frederick of Whitenberg and thought him quite a pleasant, if rather stupid, man.

He remembered he had visited Whitenberg.

It had been at least three years ago, and there had been a sturdy, somewhat plain girl amongst the Grand Duke's large family of sons.

He had taken no particular notice of her at the time.

It had never occurred to him for one moment that his Mother might try to arrange a marriage for him at his age.

He had refused so often even to contemplate taking such a step.

That it should be with the Princess Helgie of Whitenberg made it even worse.

He was well aware of the stiff protocol that was observed in that small German Principality.

The Family of the Grand Duke was restricted from enjoying any of the pursuits which were available to the younger members of the English Royal Family.

The two days the Marquis had stayed at the Palace of the Grand Duke had bored him to distraction.

He could imagine nothing worse than having to spend many more days than that in a Palace where, when the Grand Duke spoke, everybody listened attentively in silence.

The Marquis drew in his breath.

He was just about to say that nothing would induce

him to marry Princess Helgie, when his Mother said in a faltering voice:

"It would . . . make me so . . . happy, Dearest, for you to . . . settle down and have an . . . heir. You are . . . over thirty . . . and as Sir William has said . . . I must be very careful if I am to . . . live to see my . . . grandchildren."

With difficulty, the Marquis bit back the words that trembled on his lips.

Forcing himself to speak calmly, he said:

"This has certainly come as a shock, Mama, but I hope to have the chance of meeting the Princess before it is formally accepted that I should marry her."

"Of course, of course!" the Marchioness said too quickly. "It is just that I have asked her to stay here with her Mother. But she will also attend a few parties in London. So if you will invite her, she can stay with you at Lyn House."

The Marquis realised that this would set the seal more firmly than anything else on the marriage contract.

"I think that would be a mistake, Mama . . ." he began.

The Marchioness gave a little cry.

"Oh, please, Dearest Vernon, do not make difficulties! I have set my heart on your meeting Helgie and I know you will fall in love with her. You will have a beautiful wedding—I must try to be on my feet for that—and if I have to die, then I shall die happy!"

The Marquis knew he could not argue with his Mother at this moment when she seemed so frail.

Because it meant so much to her, there were tears in her eyes.

Again with difficulty, he asked calmly:

"When is this visit to take place?"

"The Grand Duke has written to say that Princess Helgie and her Mother will be with me ten days from now. She will stay here first, when I will ask all our friends to welcome them in London. Then they will move to Lyn House."

The Marquis's lips tightened, but he said:

"You seem to have it all planned out, Mama!"

The Marchioness smiled.

"Your Father always said you got your organising ability from me. I pride myself that I have, in fact, found a wife who is worthy of you, and of course of the position she will hold."

The Marquis rose from the bed and walked towards the window.

He stood looking out onto the garden, which seemed for the moment to be a pit of darkness.

His Mother was closing the prison-walls around him.

It would be impossible for him to escape without causing a scandal.

To insult a minor Royalty would be to bring down the wrath of Queen Victoria on his head.

There was, therefore, nothing he could do but propose marriage to Princess Helgie almost as soon as she arrived.

Without turning round, he said aloud:

"I thought you said this was an arrangement just between you and the Grand Duke, but if he has asked the advice of his Statesmen, it will already be public knowledge in Whitenberg."

"No, no, of course not," the Marchioness replied. "The Grand Duke told me in his letter and he gave me his word before he left, that he had discussed it only in a general manner with his Cabinet."

The Marquis still did not move, and she went on:

"I am sure that he did not give any names, but merely asked them if it was possible, as her brother had married a commoner, for Princess Helgie to marry a member of the English nobility, who are only one step below the Royal Family."

The Marquis thought this version was only his Mother's idea of what had taken place.

He hoped it was the truth.

It was, however, something of which he could not be sure.

Looking out of the window with unseeing eyes, he was thinking that he was trapped.

No-one except his Mother could have done it so skilfully.

"I expected that you might be upset at my interfering, Dearest," the Marchioness said after a long pause, "but I cannot think of anyone who is not Royal who is good enough for you, and I know your Father would have felt the same."

"I personally have never given myself such airs and graces," the Marquis said sharply.

Then, because he was afraid his Mother might be hurt, he turned round.

"I am sure what you have done you thought was for the best," he said, "but it has come as a shock, and you know I have no wish to marry anyone!"

"I know, Dearest," the Marchioness replied, "but Lady Maxwell is doing so much harm to your reputation that it is something which makes me very unhappy."

"Harm?" the Marquis enquired. "What do you mean by harm?"

"Oh, Dearest, she talks openly about you, and your Aunt has told me she is telling everyone how desperately and over-whelmingly in love she is with you."

The Marchioness's voice sharpened as she went on:

"No-one with any sensibility and good blood would talk in such a way, and I cannot bear it where you are concerned."

She put out her hand before she added:

"I cannot have you harmed by this tiresome, gossiping woman. When I was a girl, it was considered very bad form to talk about one's love-affairs."

"It still is!" the Marquis said.

He was thinking, as he spoke, that Lady Maxwell had definitely been a mistake.

He had thought so last night.

He knew now that he should have dropped her long ago, when she had first begun to cling to him in public.

The Marquis was, however, too accustomed to women looking at him with adoring eyes.

He had, in fact, been beguiled by Lady Maxwell's beauty into believing that she would behave as was expected of any woman in her position.

From the first moment she started deviating from what was called "proper behaviour" he should have discarded her.

Instead, while he had remonstrated her, it was difficult to resist the manner in which she told him with unmistakable passion that she adored him.

"I love you, I love you, Vernon!" she had said over and over again. "How can you be so wonderful, so clever, so brilliant, and yet still be a human being?"

There was no doubt of her sincerity in speaking so emotionally.

She also looked very lovely as she did so.

So, instead of warning her to be more discreet, he had kissed her.

Now, when he least expected it, she had precipitated his Mother, of all people, into taking hasty action.

"You see, Darling," the Marchioness was saying in her soft voice, "ever since you grew up, women have fallen in love with you, but there has never been any real scandal of the type this Lady Maxwell is likely to cause."

"That is nonsense!" the Marquis protested.

"It is inevitable if she talks so much," his Mother insisted. "Your Aunt thinks it is only a question of time before Queen Victoria gets to hear of it. Her Majesty would be extremely annoyed, considering that Lord Maxwell has a very important position at Court."

The Marquis could not argue with that.

Once again, he cursed himself for having let things go so far.

He wondered, if he promised to drop Lady Maxwell immediately, whether his Mother might forget her idea of his marrying Princess Helgie.

Then he knew it would only distress her.

Having invited the Princess to stay, she could hardly write and say that she had changed her mind.

As if she were following his thoughts, the Marchioness said:

"You will see, my precious Son, it will all work out for the best. I want you to marry someone whose blood is the equal of ours, and who will grace the position that I have held for so long as the Chatelaine of Lyn."

"You have certainly graced it, Mama," the Marquis said automatically.

"Your Father was very proud of me, and I would no more have caused a scandal that might upset him than fly over the moon!"

"No, of course not," the Marquis agreed. "You were a perfect wife, just as you have always been a perfect Mother to me."

"Oh, Dearest, that is just what I wanted you to say," the Marchioness exclaimed. "When you were a little boy I used to tell you that 'Mother knows best,' and you must believe me when I say now that I know best about this."

The Marquis did not answer.

He merely walked back to the bed, and sat down where he had sat before.

"You have certainly given me something to think about, Mama," he said, "but now I want you to think about yourself. You must do exactly what Sir William says, and I shall ask him to report to me every time he comes to see you. I shall be very angry if you are doing too much, or getting unnecessarily tired."

"I will not do that," the Marchioness said, "but I want to be well enough to get up and entertain the Princess, and you must promise me that you will have no engagements for that week."

She paused before she added:

"When she moves to your house, you must ask everyone who you know will be congenial to meet her."

The Marquis did not answer.

He was merely thinking that most of his friends would find Whitenberg as dull as he had.

He kissed his Mother.

"I am sure you have arranged luncheon for me downstairs," he said, "and I will go outside and look at the garden to see that the gardeners are providing you with sufficient fruit and vegetables."

"They are all longing to see you, Dearest," his Mother said, "and do not forget Mrs. Wiggins in the kitchen. She would be very disappointed and upset if you left without seeing her."

"I remember Mrs. Wiggins." The Marquis smiled. "She used to make me those delicious brandy-snaps when I was a little boy."

The Marchioness laughed.

"I expect you will have them for luncheon. Mrs. Wiggins never forgets your favourite food."

The Marquis kissed his Mother again and turned towards the door.

When he went downstairs, he went into the garden.

He walked across the green lawns, which sloped down to the river.

He was thinking that if it had come from his greatest enemy, he could not have received more appalling or horrifying news than what he had heard from his Mother.

He stood looking down into the river.

The ducks, which his Mother bred, swam round, hoping he would feed them.

All he could see were the long years of boredom ahead of him, the dull conversation to which he had listened when he had visited Whitenberg.

Then he saw the plain face of the Princess as a child.

He wondered if she was now better looking with the years, but doubted it.

Even if her looks had improved, it was unlikely that, as her Father's and Mother's daughter, her intelligence would in any way exceed theirs.

"I cannot do it! I cannot!" the Marquis said aloud.

* * *

Driving back to London, the Marquis remembered that he had the problem of Lady Maxwell which was still unsolved.

It was bad enough to think that he had only ten days of freedom without having to spend hours, and perhaps days, of it with Joan Maxwell.

She would be crying and pleading with him not to leave her.

He knew from past experience that there would be tears and recriminations, and incessant cries of:

"What have I done? Why do you no longer love me? Why? Why? Why?"

He had heard it all a hundred times.

Every nerve in his body shrank from being involved in what he knew would be a pointless, tempestuous, and degrading scene.

Only when he got back to his house did he find a solution.

He walked straight into his Study.

Perhaps, he thought, there would be some urgent messages for him because he had been away all day.

He was not mistaken.

There were quite a number lying on top of his blotter.

The first that he saw was another note marked *VERY URGENT*.

He knew it was from Joan Maxwell.

Because it was like touching a raw nerve, he turned from his desk towards the fireplace.

In front of it, carefully arranged on a low stool, were the newspapers.

Automatically, remembering he had not seen one all day, the Marquis picked up *The Morning Post*.

He opened it, not really interested in what he read.

He only wanted to take his thoughts away from the note lying on the blotter and from his Mother's voice, still ringing in his ears.

It was then under FOREIGN AFFAIRS, that without really thinking, he read:

**"RITZ HOTEL TO BE OPENED IN PARIS ON THURSDAY.
SOCIETY FLOCKS TO THE PLACE VENDÔME.
CÉSAR RITZ GREATEST HOTELIER IN EUROPE."**

The Marquis read the headlines.

Then something seemed to snap in his mind.

"I will go to Paris," he decided, "tomorrow morning!"

chapter three

THE Marquis spent much of the time on his journey to Paris worrying about the future.

He was also trying to plan how he could enjoy himself in Paris.

But it was impossible not to feel depressed.

He had been there on numerous occasions, the first time being when he had just left Oxford.

He and a friend had then sampled the delights of the gayest City in the world.

Paris to him always meant amusement: a *joie de vivre* which he did not find in England.

The train quickly gathered speed from Calais.

As it carried him towards Paris, he was wondering which of the many Courtesans whom he had known in the past he would seek out now.

There were no women in the whole world as exotic and amusing as the *cocottes* of Paris.

They emptied a man's pockets, but he enjoyed their

company so much that he did not even think of the expense.

Quite a number had passed through the Marquis's hands.

Each had had some special attraction of her own.

Then he told himself he would leave it to Fate and see who he encountered at Maxim's.

Maxim's Restaurant was a *rendez-vous* for all men who wished to enjoy the special pleasures of Paris.

Mr. Butterworth had sent a telegram to the Ritz Hotel announcing the Marquis's arrival.

He was not surprised when he eventually reached the *Place Vendôme* to find César Ritz himself waiting to receive him.

"It is a great honour, M'Lord," he said, "and my party tonight would not be complete without you."

The Marquis shook him by the hand and wished him luck.

At the same time, he was not particularly eager to take part in the opening festivities.

He knew he would find there both French and English friends who would expect to entertain him afterwards.

César Ritz took him up the stairs to the Suite he had reserved for him.

Before he dressed, the Marquis told him that he had a prior engagement for that evening.

"That is very sad for me, My Lord," César Ritz said. "I am overwhelmed by the people who have accepted my invitation, but I kept a special place for you."

"I want to enjoy your magnificent Hotel," the Marquis answered, "without being disturbed by the chatter of people I see too often in England, and, hopefully too little in France."

César Ritz laughed.

"This I understand, My Lord, and tomorrow you shall enjoy the finest dinner you have ever eaten or my Chefs have ever cooked."

The Marquis had a bath in the bathroom, which opened out of his bedroom.

He appreciated the gold fittings, the mirrors, and the profusion of toilet facilities which were provided.

As he went downstairs, the guests were already assembling.

The Marquis decided he had no wish to meet the Marlboroughs or the Portlands.

He had learnt from the newspapers they were staying at the hotel.

Nor did he wish to encounter the *Duchesse* de Morny, who was very lovely, but would be with her husband.

The same applied to the *Duchesse* de Rohan, whom he had known in the past.

Instead, he dined at Maxim's.

As usual, it was full of men, like himself, looking for amusement, and the most notorious and expensive *cocottes* in Paris.

The Marquis attached himself to a very attractive one.

She was only too willing to exploit all her arts for his delectation.

She was certainly extremely alluring.

When he returned to the Ritz as dawn was breaking, he knew that for a few hours at any rate she had made him forget the future.

He was awoken by Barker telling him what an enormous success the party last night had been.

The valet was quite voluble about it.

The Marquis knew to his amusement that Barker was upset that his Master had missed such a treat.

The Marquis dressed slowly.

He decided he would drive in the *Bois*.

Lisette, before he had left her last night, had suggested that she would enjoy being with him if he picked her up at noon.

He therefore drove to her elegant house.

It was situated in a discreet road not far from the *Arc de Triomphe*.

A maid-servant in a frilly uniform let him in and indicated that *Madame* was waiting for him in her bedroom.

The Marquis, therefore, climbed the stairs he had descended not many hours before.

He found Lisette sitting in front of her mirror applying mascara to her eye-lashes.

"Bonjour, mon brave!" she said. "You are happy today?"

"You made me very happy last night," the Marquis answered. "I thought, as you suggested, that we might drive together in the *Bois*."

"Of course, I would love to do that," Lisette replied, "and who else could have such a handsome and distinguished escort as I will?"

She gave the Marquis her hand, and he kissed it.

At the same time, he thought the bedroom was rather stuffy and Lisette's perfume slightly overpowering.

"I will wait downstairs," he said.

"But, of course," she replied, "and there is champagne in the Drawing-Room."

It was typical, the Marquis thought with a smile, that a French *cocotte* should have champagne waiting in a silver ice-cooler.

It was of the finest vintage and there were small *pâté* sandwiches for him to eat.

He was, however, not hungry, because he had eaten an excellent breakfast at the Ritz.

He looked about him.

The huge basket of flowers on the table and in the fireplace, and the windows open to let in the fresh air, made a delightful scene.

He knew that when Lisette appeared she would be exquisitely dressed and bejewelled.

Her face would be powdered and painted.

No man would ever see her unless she was looking her best.

He thought it was something a wife would never understand.

He remembered how unattractive his bedroom was when he had stayed at the Palace in Whitenberg.

He had thought, too, that the furnishings in every room were dull, heavy, and almost dingy.

The curtains were festooned with frills and fringes, every sofa was covered in velvet or some other heavy material.

He had a sudden horror that any woman, once she bore his name, would want to alter Lyn.

It was perfect as it was, he told himself.

He knew that even the Prince of Wales was envious of the comfort and the elegance he found there.

The rooms were furnished in the perfect taste that had been sponsored in the Regency period by the Prince of Wales, later George IV.

The Marquis was quite certain that Princess Helgie would favour the Victorian invasion of antimacassars, together with all the jumble of frills and furbelows, which to his eyes were appallingly ugly.

Perhaps, like the Queen, she would want to display hundreds of photographs of her relatives.

She might even demand aspidistras, which he had sworn never to have in any of his houses.

Because just to think of the Princess was to upset him, he was thankful when, a few minutes later, Lisette joined him.

She was looking, he thought, exceedingly *chic*.

Her tight-fitting gown accentuated her tiny waist and the curves of her breasts.

There was no mistaking that she was anything but what she was.

The Marquis was, for the moment, shying away from anything that could be called "ladylike."

Lisette walked towards him.

Then she swung round so that her skirt swirled out, betraying her lace-edged petticoats.

"How do I look?" she asked, speaking in the fascinating and caressing tone which no man could resist. "Do I please you?"

"You please me very much," the Marquis answered, "and now let me show you off to all those men in the *Bois* who will be envying me for having you by my side."

"As the women will want to scratch out my eyes because I am with you!" Lisette laughed.

She gave him a provocative glance from under her long eye-lashes.

The Marquis was smiling as they walked down the steps.

He helped her into the Chaise he had hired from the Livery Stables he always used when he came to Paris.

They had the most up-to-date carriages and the best-bred horses.

He knew they would never provide for him anything that was second-rate.

The horses he was driving were an exceptionally fine pair.

The Chaise, like one of its present occupants, was somewhat flamboyant, which suited the Marquis's mood.

The sun was shining.

The *Bois* was crowded with Gentlemen on horseback and carriages filled with all the most famous *cocottes* in Paris.

Each one had some individual way of advertising herself.

This custom was uniquely French and not to be found in any other City.

One *cocotte*'s turn-out was altogether white, her horses, her carriages, and the clothes she wore.

Another equally famous Courtesan had two large poodles with their coats dyed blue, and wearing collars studded with real jewels.

They sat opposite her with their backs to the horses.

She had more ospreys in her hat than any other woman.

Her rope of pearls, which were reputed to have been given to her by a King, reached down to her knees.

She drove alone except for her dogs. No man was ever invited to accompany her in the *Bois*.

Some of the outstanding Courtesans the Marquis had known in the past.

There were also some newcomers whom Lisette pointed out to him.

About each one she made amusing, if slightly spiteful, remarks.

When they stopped for luncheon the Marquis realised that he had been laughing most of the morning.

Once again he had forgotten the future.

After luncheon they went back to Lisette's house, and he made love to her before returning to the Ritz.

"Will you dine with me tonight, Lisette?" he asked as he dressed himself.

He was standing in front of her elaborate mirror framed with gold and embellished by Cupids.

"Alas, *mon cher,* while I would like it more than anything, I already have promised to attend a party which had been arranged for a long time. I would, of course, be very happy if you would come with me."

The Marquis shook his head.

"I am not looking for parties in Paris at the moment, and if you cannot dine with me, I would prefer to dine alone."

"As long as it is alone!" Lisette said. "I feel very jealous at the thought that you could fill my place very easily."

"That would be impossible," the Marquis replied gallantly.

He thought, however, when he left Lisette's house, that enough was enough.

Lisette was one of the most attractive of her profession.

Yet it would be a mistake to overdo even the most succulent helping of *pâté de foie gras.*

"I will dine alone," he told himself, "and concentrate on the food. I am sure there are some new dishes in Paris, which I shall insist on my Chef attempting when I am next at Lyn."

He handed the reins of the Chaise to the groom, and walked into the Ritz Hotel.

Because he was well-known, the Concierge bowed to him as he passed the desk.

He walked slowly towards the curving staircase.

He noticed that people were still coming from the Dining-Room.

Others, smartly dressed, were congregating where afternoon-tea was served.

He had no wish to encounter any of his friends.

They would inevitably ask him why he was in Paris in the middle of the London Season.

He quickened his pace so as not to be seen.

Then he walked slowly along the corridor leading to his Suite.

When he had nearly reached his own rooms he heard a woman's voice cry out in English:

"Help me . . . somebody! Oh . . . please . . . help me!"

It was so obviously a cry that came from the heart that the Marquis paused.

He glanced through the open door from which the cry had come.

He saw to his surprise, the *Comte* Gaston de Forêt.

He was an old enemy, and the Marquis was delighted at the opportunity of rescuing someone from his clutches.

He had in fact crossed the *Comte*'s path on several occasions.

Each of them had instinctively resented the other from the moment they were first introduced.

The last time the Marquis was in Paris he had snatched from under the *Comte*'s nose a very attractive actress.

Yvonne had just become a success at the *Folies Bergère*.

Although she had appeared in the Provinces, this was the first time she had graced a Parisian stage.

There were a great number of men eager to become her Protector.

But, with the typical good sense of a Frenchwoman, Yvonne was taking her time in making up her mind whom she should choose.

The *Comte* de Forêt was obviously the most important of her admirers, and certainly the richest.

She had permitted him to take her out to supper on several occasions.

But she had not yet surrendered to his ardour.

He had offered her an apartment, which was in a more expensive district than where she was living at the moment.

Still she had not accepted.

When the Marquis appeared, the *Comte* was immediately forgotten and he was furious.

He raged at the Marquis, who had swept the little actress off her feet and into his arms.

The Marquis laughed, and spent a month in Paris when he had intended to be there for only a few days.

He found it very enjoyable.

When he left, Yvonne against all the rules, had wept and clung to him, saying:

"How can I let you go? Nothing will be the same when you are no longer here."

"You know I have to return to my own country, where I have a great many things to attend to," the Marquis explained, "but I will never forget what an enjoyable month this has been."

"And I shall never forget you!" Yvonne sobbed.

As the Marquis travelled back to England, he had thought of his attractive *protégée*.

But he knew that one part of his brain was telling him it was time to go back to his duties and his horses.

Friends in London were also awaiting him, men of distinction in Politics, Arts, and in Sport.

There would be women, of course, there were always women in his life.

At the same time, he knew he was looking forward to talking to the Secretary of State for Foreign Affairs, and to the hours he would spend discussing horses with the Members of the Jockey Club.

"Enough is enough" was something he had said a great number of times in his life.

Only a few days after his return, Paris was a thing of the past.

Everything that was important and interesting was English and in the present.

Now, as he saw the anger on the *Comte*'s face at his appearance, the memory of Yvonne came back to him.

He could understand how frustrated the Frenchman had been.

He was not surprised now to find that Gaston de Forêt was forcing himself on another very pretty, in fact, quite lovely, young woman.

She was standing on a ladder.

As he and the *Comte* exchanged words, she slipped down from it with a quickness he commended.

She reached him in the doorway.

When he took her away, he was aware that she was trembling, and also that she was very young.

Then she remembered that she had left her hat behind.

The Marquis thought with amusement that it would give him a chance to tell the *Comte* once again what he thought of him.

He had always disliked de Forêt.

He could understand that to a young Englishwoman who was not used to the kind of compliments the *Comte* would pay her, he could seem terrifying.

As he shut Vilma into his Sitting-Room, the Marquis walked slowly back to the *Comte*'s.

He was standing where they had left him, obviously still in a rage.

As the Marquis entered, the *Comte* enquired in French:

"In God's name, what do you want now?"

"Nothing more expensive than the lady's hat which is on that chair," the Marquis replied.

The *Comte* looked round, saw Vilma's hat, and said sharply:

"You are taking nothing from here! If the young woman wants her belongings, she can come to fetch them herself!"

"And you really think you can stop me from assisting her as I am determined to do?" the Marquis enquired.

He walked to the chair as he spoke and picked up the hat.

He realised as he did so that the *Comte* had clenched his fists.

"I think that as a pugilist you are not really up to scratch!" he said coolly.

As the Marquis was both taller and heavier, it was what the *Comte* was thinking himself.

He shrugged his shoulders, turned away, and walked to the window.

"Get out, Lynworth," he shouted, "and stay out! I have always hoped I should never have the unpleasantness of meeting you again."

"The wish is mutual," the Marquis replied, "and I suggest that you keep away from young English girls who do not understand the perverted tastes of a foreigner like yourself."

The contemptuous way he spoke made the *Comte* so angry that he could only make a rude sound.

The Marquis laughed as he walked down the corridor carrying Vilma's hat.

When he entered the Sitting-Room he saw her lying back in one of the armchairs, and realised she was in a state of shock.

She was very pale.

When she heard him come into the room, she sat up quickly, as if she were still afraid.

"It is all right," the Marquis said. "Here is your hat, although the *Comte* had no wish to part with it."

"Th-thank . . . you," Vilma managed to murmur.

She would have got out of the chair, but the Marquis put out his hand to prevent her.

"I suggest," he said, "that you rest here for a few minutes, otherwise you might run into the *Comte* who is behaving like a ferocious tiger deprived of its prey!"

He tried to speak lightly and make Vilma laugh.

Instead, she clasped her hands together and he could see the fear in her eyes.

"I will tell you what I am going to do," he went on. "I see there is a bottle of champagne on the table with the compliments of César Ritz. It will not be as cold as it should be, but you and I will have a glass of it, and I am sure it will make you feel better."

He did not wait for Vilma to reply.

He opened the champagne and poured some into two glasses that were also on the table, together with a bowl of fruit.

The Marquis picked up one of the glasses and carried it to Vilma.

"I . . . I do not think . . . I should . . . drink . . . at this . . ." she began a little hesitatingly.

"Nonsense!" the Marquis interrupted. "You are now in Paris, and champagne can be drunk here at any time of the day or night, especially when you are in need of it."

Vilma gave a little choked laugh.

"It does seem very French to be drinking it at this time of . . . the afternoon when . . . one should be having a . . . cup of . . . tea."

"Not in Paris!" the Marquis said.

"I know that . . . and thank you. It was silly of me to be so . . . frightened."

"As a matter of fact, it was very sensible," the Marquis replied. "Let me tell you that *Comte* Gaston de Forêt is someone you should avoid wherever you may meet him."

He drew a chair up beside her and asked:

"Are you really, looking as you do, an expert in electricity?"

"I do know . . . a little . . . about it," Vilma admitted.

She was thinking that perhaps it was a good thing that the Marquis should assume she was an employee of *Monsieur* Ritz.

Her Father, however, would be furious if he knew that she had been insulted by the *Comte* de Forêt.

And now she was sipping champagne in the Marquis's private rooms.

"Suppose you tell me your name?" the Marquis was saying. "Then we shall have been formally introduced."

"My name is Vilma."

"Is that all?"

"No."

For a moment Vilma thought of inventing a name. Then she told herself that "Crawshaw" would mean nothing to him, and he must never know who she really was.

"My surname is Crawshaw," she said aloud.

"And I am the Marquis of Lynworth," he answered. "As you are English, you may have heard of my race-horses."

"Of course I have," Vilma cried. "I know *Starlight* won the Derby this year."

"That was a great triumph for me, and I was very proud of it," the Marquis replied. "Are you living in Paris?"

"No, I am only . . . staying here for a . . . short time," Vilma replied.

"I have a feeling that César Ritz asked you to help in his arrangement of the chandeliers because he suspected that the English might be more advanced in electricity than the French."

"I think it is really the . . . other way . . . around," Vilma replied.

"Then of course I must bow to your superior knowledge." The Marquis smiled. "I have put a little electricity into my house in England, but I have thought since coming here that César Ritz's lighting is in many ways superior."

"That is because the colour he has chosen is a pale apricot pink," Vilma said. "He told me he spent hours and hours experimenting so as to make it becoming to a woman's complexion."

The Marquis laughed.

"Only a Frenchman would think like that, and I admit it is something that had never occurred to me."

Vilma took another sip of her champagne, then put it down with the glass still quite full.

"I think I should . . . go now," she said.

"Must you be in such a hurry?" the Marquis asked. "There are a lot of things I want to ask you. For instance, I am sure you can help me solve the problem of my antique silver sconces which I know will be difficult to wire."

Vilma thought she was certainly getting out of her depth, and she said quickly:

"*Monsieur* Ritz has a most experienced Electrician who had wired the chandelier in the *Comte*'s room. He only went away to get some light-bulbs. He should be back any time now."

"I think I should leave him to finish the job, without upsetting the *Comte* any further," the Marquis said. "When he has finished, the door will be shut, and then it will be safe for you to go past it."

Vilma knew she had no wish to encounter the *Comte* again.

She gave a little shiver, which the Marquis did not miss.

He drank more of his champagne before he said:

"Surely you are not walking about Paris alone? If you are, I am sure you will get into all sorts of trouble."

"I was not alone when I came here, because *Mon-*

sieur Ritz was kind enough to bring me from where I am staying. He must be looking for me by now."

She felt as she spoke that it was now firmly in the Marquis's mind that she had something to do with the electricity.

In fact, his next words showed her that she was not mistaken.

"As you have finished your work for today," he said, "you can now relax, and we will talk of things that interest us both."

Vilma gave a little laugh.

"You mean horses!"

"Of course," the Marquis said, his eyes twinkling. "What else would two English people talk about?"

"Tell me about the horses you think will win," Vilma begged.

The Marquis told her about those he had in training.

He realised as he spoke that she was genuinely interested.

He had found that most women took the trouble to congratulate him on his wins, yet if he tried to discuss form and breeding, they very quickly got the conversation back to themselves.

Vilma was different.

He soon realised she knew a great deal about horses and the breeding of them.

She was fascinated by everything he was prepared to tell her.

He rose to fill up her glass.

As if he had broken the spell that seemed to have existed between them, she said:

"I really must go now. My Father is not well, and I do not like to leave him for long."

"I am sorry to hear that," the Marquis said. "I was just wondering if we could continue this conversation at dinner."

Vilma stared at him in astonishment.

He knew it was something she had not expected him to suggest.

"We will not dine here if that will embarrass you," he said, "but I know of a charming little place on the Left Bank where the food is delicious and we shall neither of us see anybody we know."

"It is . . . very kind of you, but of course it is . . . something I . . . cannot do."

"Why not?" the Marquis asked.

As he asked the question, he knew she was struggling to think of an answer.

She knew that it would be very exciting to dine alone with a man in Paris.

It was, however, something unthinkable for a *débutante* to do.

"I have a feeling," the Marquis was saying, "that you have not been staying in Paris for long and you have not seen it at night."

She looked at him questioningly, but she did not speak, and he went on:

"I would like to drive with you along the Seine. To me nothing is more beautiful than the *Place de la Concorde* with the fountains playing and the stars overhead."

Vilma drew in her breath.

This was what she herself longed to see.

And she knew that no-one else would offer to take her.

"Could I . . . really do . . . that?" she asked.

She was asking herself rather than the Marquis.

"I promise you," he said, "that I shall take you home immediately when you want me to. It is something I shall much enjoy seeing myself, and I want to show it to you for the first time."

Vilma hesitated and was lost.

"Do you . . . really think it . . . would be all . . . right?" she asked. "I could get . . . away by . . . nine o'clock."

She knew by that time her Father would have had his dinner.

After that he would have to be quiet and go to sleep.

"It will suit me admirably," the Marquis said. "Where shall I meet you?"

That, Vilma thought, was undoubtedly a problem.

If she asked him to come to the house where she was staying, he might know the *Vicomte*.

Apart from that, Herbert would undoubtedly tell her Father that she had been collected.

"Could I," she asked, "meet you here at the . . . back door?"

"Of course, if that is what you prefer," the Marquis said.

He thought to himself that perhaps she was ashamed of where she was staying.

Perhaps she was, in fact, very poor.

At the same time, his experienced eye knew that her gown, which fitted her perfectly, was an expensive one.

She was becoming a mystery.

If there was one thing the Marquis enjoyed, it was something that was unexpected and surprised him.

Aloud he said:

"I will be downstairs waiting at the 'back door,' as

you call it, at nine o'clock. I promise you, there will be no dragons to frighten you! Need I say I am looking forward to our evening together enormously?"

"Thank you, thank you," Vilma said. "And now, if you will be kind enough just to look and see if the door of the *Comte*'s room is closed, I will go to find *Monsieur* Ritz."

She held out her hand, and the Marquis shook it.

Then she picked up her hat and put it on her head, giving her reflection in the mirror only a quick glance.

Watching her, the Marquis thought her unself-consciousness was very attractive.

She was certainly very different from any woman he had ever known.

"It is because she is so young," he told himself, "and far too pretty to be roaming about Paris on her own."

He thought it was very remiss of her family, if she had one, not to take more care of her.

He said nothing, and as she turned towards the door, he opened it.

He looked outside.

All the doors along the corridor were closed, and he said:

"You are quite safe, but I should hurry!"

Vilma smiled at him.

"You have been . . . very kind, but please . . . just watch until I reach the end of the corridor . . . in case the *Comte* comes out from his room."

She was speaking nervously.

The Marquis knew her fear of the *Comte* was genuine.

"I shall watch you until you are out of sight," he promised.

Vilma set off down the corridor, moving so swiftly that the Marquis felt as if her feet barely touched the floor.

He watched her until she was just a very small figure at the end of it.

Then, as he expected, she turned back and raised her hand.

She did not linger, but disappeared.

chapter four

AS she reached the side-staircase by which she had ascended, Vilma saw César Ritz hurrying up it.

She waited until, as he reached the top, he saw her, and exclaimed:

"Oh, *Mademoiselle,* I am so sorry. You must forgive me. But there has been a muddle and only I could sort it out."

"I can quite believe that," Vilma replied, "but now, *Monsieur,* I must go home."

He glanced along the corridor as if he were surprised, and she added:

"The *Comte* Gaston de Forêt has arrived."

"Arrived?" *Monsieur* Ritz exclaimed. "He told me he would not be here until seven o'clock!"

Vilma did not reply.

She merely started to walk down the stairs.

César Ritz, grumbling beneath his breath, followed her.

His carriage was waiting there.

He helped her into it and got in himself beside her.

As he did so, Vilma exclaimed:

"I am sure, *Monsieur,* you have so much to do in the Hotel and I could go back alone."

"That would not be *comme il faut,*" he replied severely. "You have done me a great favour, so how could I do anything but be respectful and escort you safely back to the *Vicomte*'s house?"

Vilma did not answer.

She was thinking how shocked César Ritz would be if he learnt how the *Comte* had behaved.

'It was very lucky,' she thought, 'that the Marquis was passing the open door. Otherwise he might have . . . kissed me.'

She shivered again at the idea, then forced herself to concentrate on what César Ritz was saying.

He was giving her a list of the guests who had had luncheon at the Ritz, and those who had booked tables for dinner this evening.

They sounded very distinguished, and Vilma would have liked to see them all at dinner.

But she thought it was more exciting, though wrong of her, to be going to dine with the Marquis.

When the carriage arrived back at the *Vicomte*'s house, she thanked César Ritz for taking her to his Hotel.

He thanked her again for the chandelier.

When she went into the house, Herbert was outside her Father's door, and she asked:

"How is Papa? Will he see me now?"

" 'Is Lordship . . . I mean th' Colonel, is asleep," Herbert replied, "an' I thinks it's th' best thing for 'im after 'is treatment."

"I only hope it is really doing him good," Vilma said.

"That man Blanc's famous, I understands," Herbert said, "an' th' sooner we can get back t' England, th' better!"

Vilma did not reply.

She was thinking it was very thrilling to be in Paris, especially tonight, when she would see it under the stars.

She lay on her bed and read a book.

Later, Herbert came to tell her that her Father was awake and he was going to the Kitchen to order something for him to eat.

Vilma ran along the corridor to her Father's room.

He was, she thought, looking pale, and he smiled at her as she came to his bedside.

"How are you, Papa?" she asked.

"I am tired," the Earl replied. "At the same time, the pain in my back is not as bad as it was."

Vilma gave a little cry of joy.

"Oh, Papa, that is what I want to hear! But you must rest, as *Monsieur* Blanc insists, and not worry about anything."

She sat with him while he had a little soup and a few mouthfuls of fish.

Then he pushed the plate away, saying:

"I have no wish to eat any more. In fact, I am so tired, I must go to sleep."

Herbert took away the tray, and Vilma kissed her Father good-night.

"I am sure you will feel better in the morning, Papa," she said.

"I hope so," the Earl answered. "I would like to

show you Paris, but it is impossible in the condition I am in now."

"Of course it is, Papa. Just do not worry about anything but getting well," Vilma said.

As she went back to her own room, she felt guilty.

But how could she resist seeing a little of Paris?

Besides, she was quite certain the Marquis would look after her properly.

She put on a pretty and expensive gown and covered it with a velvet cloak that was the colour of sapphires.

It made her skin look dazzlingly white.

She looked at herself in the mirror anxiously.

She hoped the Marquis would not think her dull and dowdy beside the smartly dressed and *chic* Frenchwomen.

As she went downstairs, she was turning over in her mind what was the best way of getting to the Ritz.

She did not want the servants to think it a strange thing for her to do.

When she saw the old Butler in the Hall she said to him:

"I am dining with some friends, and I said I would meet them in the *Rue Cambon*. Will you please call me a *fiacre*, and do you think you could send one of the housemaids with me."

"I'll come myself, *M'mselle,*" the Butler replied.

"No, no, that would be too much when you have so many other things to do," Vilma answered. "I am sure Marie would enjoy the drive."

Marie was the middle-aged maid who looked after her.

The Butler accepted her decision and sent one of the footmen to call a *fiacre*.

He himself collected Marie from the Kitchen.

By the time she had found a bonnet and shawl to go over her shoulders, the *fiacre* was at the door.

Vilma stepped into it.

She told the coachman the number of the house in the *Rue Cambon.*

She hoped the old Butler would not recognise it as the back door of the Ritz.

They drove off, and Marie said:

"This is a real treat for me, *M'mselle.* I've often thought I'd rather drive than walk, but *voitures* in Paris are too expensive for the likes of me."

"Then you must accompany me tomorrow when I go shopping," Vilma replied.

Marie was obviously delighted at this.

Vilma thought it would take her mind off where they were going and with whom she was dining.

She was quite sure that the French servants would be no less inquisitive about her than the English servants were in England.

The one thing she had to avoid was that they should go tittle-tattling about it to her Father.

'I shall tell Papa eventually about the Marquis,' she thought, 'but it would make him very upset at the moment. I am quite sure Papa has met him on the race-course and that he is one of the people Papa would not wish to know about his fall.'

The *fiacre* drew up outside the back door of the Ritz.

Vilma was worried to see several Gentlemen in evening-dress going in ahead of her.

She had not expected that quite a number of people would use this door as well as the main entrance in the *Place Vendôme.*

She gave Marie some money to pay the cabman.

As she alighted she told him to return to the house from which they had come.

As he drove away she walked rather shyly, feeling alarmingly conspicuous, up the steps and in through the door.

There was a small Hall inside, in no way as impressive as the one at the front of the Hotel.

There were, however, comfortable chairs and beautiful arrangements of flowers.

To her relief, she saw the Marquis, and as she hurried towards him, he said:

"You are punctual, which is unusual for a lovely woman!"

It was the sort of remark he would have made to anyone with whom he was dining.

He was surprised, therefore, when Vilma blushed.

"My carriage is waiting outside," he said, "unless you wish to join the crowd who are flocking into the Dining-Room here. Personally I think the sooner we are on our way, the better."

"Yes, please, let us go at once," Vilma agreed.

A few moments later they were driving away.

The Marquis leaned back comfortably against the padded seat.

But Vilma sat forward, looking excitedly out of the window at the streets which were already being lit up.

She had her profile to the Marquis, and he thought that as he had said to her, she was indeed very lovely.

As they drove along, Vilma was so enraptured by all she saw that she forgot to be polite and talk to her host.

To the Marquis it was a new experience.

He had a beautiful woman beside him who found him less attractive than the streets through which they were passing.

They drove in silence until the Marquis said:

"We are approaching the Louvre, and that is a place you must visit while you are in Paris."

"I have been thinking about that," Vilma replied, "and of course I am longing to see the pictures it contains. It is just that I have to find someone to go with me."

She said it so ingenuously that the Marquis was aware she was not asking him to escort her.

"I think what we had better do," he said, "is to make a list of all the things you want to see and I will add any others I think would interest you."

"That is very kind of you," Vilma said, "but I am not certain my Father and I will be . . . staying very . . . long."

The horses reached a bridge across the river, and she bent forward excitedly to say:

"Now I am seeing the Seine! I am sure it is even more beautiful than the eulogies which have been written about it in what must now be at least a thousand books!"

The Marquis laughed.

"Perhaps you are right, but are you telling me that you have read a great deal about Paris, even though you have not been here before?"

"Of course I have," Vilma replied. "My French Tutor used to speak of it as if to her it was Heaven on Earth."

The Marquis thought a little dryly that other people had a different idea of Paris.

It was the sort of remark he could make to a sophisticated woman, but he knew that Vilma would not understand.

On the other side of the river they drove through narrow streets, which Vilma guessed were the old part of Paris.

They finally stopped outside what appeared to be a very modest Restaurant.

The Marquis, however, was greeted effusively by the Proprietor.

They were shown to comfortable seats that were enclosed on both sides, almost like a stall for a horse.

It meant that those dining there could be private.

The ceiling and walls had a framework of wooden beams and the windows had diamond-paned casements.

"This must be a very old building!" Vilma said as they sat down.

"It was here before the Revolution," the Marquis explained. "That is why I enjoy dining here, and I thought you would appreciate it too."

"I do, I really do!" Vilma said. "It is so attractive and unusual."

The Marquis chose what they would have for dinner and ordered a bottle of champagne.

Then he said:

"Now we can talk and I want you to tell me about yourself."

"I would much rather talk about you," Vilma said, "or, rather, your horses."

"I thought we had already exhausted that subject," the Marquis remarked.

"Then tell me about your house. I was thinking as I was dressing that I saw a picture of it in one of the magazines, and I think it was built by the Adam brothers."

"You are quite right," the Marquis said, "and I have tried to keep the rooms exactly as they planned them."

"It would be terrible if you changed them," Vilma said. "I am sure you have not filled them with all the nick-nacks so beloved by this era."

"I certainly have not!" the Marquis answered firmly.

As she spoke, it flashed through his mind that that was what he was afraid the Princess would want to introduce into his house.

He told himself that, if he had to, he would fight the whole German nation.

How could he permit them to spoil what was the most perfect Palladian house in the whole of England?

"Now tell me about your pictures," Vilma said.

Almost despite himself the Marquis began to tell her about the pictures he had bought to augment the collection he had inherited.

They had finished dinner before he realised that he had talked almost incessantly about himself.

Vilma had managed to make him do so as cleverly as Lisette, the previous evening, had made him talk of love.

"It is now your turn," he said as the coffee came to the table, "to tell me what you do when you are home."

"You know the answer to that," Vilma said. "I ride, and of course until this year, I have been studying."

"I think very successfully," the Marquis remarked. "And apart from helping your Father with electricity, what do you intend to do in the future?"

Vilma thought how angry her Father would be if he heard the Marquis refer to him as a tradesman.

She just said:

"I still have a lot to learn, and I would like above all else to travel."

"What about getting married?" the Marquis asked.

"I have not thought about it," Vilma replied.

"Nonsense!" the Marquis retorted. "Every young woman dreams of marrying someone, and I am sure you already have several attentive *Beaux* who pay you compliments and bring you bouquets of flowers."

Vilma smiled.

"I have received only two bouquets of flowers," she said. "One from a dear old man who said I reminded him of his granddaughter, and the other was from somebody with whom I had danced and who wanted to see me again. But he was such a bore that I refused him."

The Marquis laughed.

"That is a very sad story, but perhaps when you return to England it will all be different. You will have acquired the French art of flirting with a man, which your English friends will find irresistible."

He was talking slightly mockingly, until he realised that Vilma was looking at him enquiringly.

"I have often wondered," she said, "what is meant by 'flirting.' I asked my Mother once, and she said it was a very vulgar way of behaving in public and something a Lady should never do."

"Then of course you must not flirt," the Marquis conceded, "but if you stay long in Paris, you may find it difficult not to do so."

"Fortunately I do not know any Frenchmen," Vilma replied, "except of course the *Comte*, and he is horrible! I still think how lucky I was that you came along and . . . saved me."

"And what do you think I saved you from?" the Marquis enquired.

Vilma blushed before she said in a low voice:

"H-he said he wanted to . . . hold me in his arms, and . . . I think he . . . would have tried to . . . kiss me."

"And would that have been so horrifying?" the Marquis asked.

"Of course it would!" Vilma declared. "He was repulsive. And I was very . . . very . . . frightened until I heard you speaking . . . English."

"I am afraid you may find a number of men like the *Comte* in Paris," the Marquis said. "But I do not want you ever to be frightened, so you must be careful about what invitations you accept."

"That is easy," Vilma murmured. "I shall not get any invitations in Paris, so I shall be quite safe."

"You accepted mine," the Marquis said a little dryly.

"But you are English," Vilma explained, "and I knew I could trust you."

"How did you know that?" the Marquis asked.

She thought for a moment before she replied:

"When one comes in contact with people, one is immediately aware of their vibrations. It is not what they say, but what you feel about them that counts."

The Marquis was surprised.

"That is what I have always believed myself," he said, "but I have never known a woman to put it so plainly."

"Sometimes I have met people whose vibrations I knew had something wrong about them, and from the moment the *Comte* spoke to me I was aware that he was menacing and dangerous."

"You must try and keep out of his way," the Marquis said. "Do you have to go to the Ritz tomorrow?"

"No, no, of course not," Vilma answered.

"Then the chandelier in the *Comte*'s bedroom is the last," the Marquis said, as if he were thinking it out for himself.

"Yes, the very last," Vilma agreed. "*Monsieur* Ritz told me himself that every room is now complete and perfect."

"Does that mean that you will now return to England?" the Marquis asked.

"I am afraid so, as soon as my Father is better."

Because she was feeling uncomfortable under this cross-examination, she managed deftly to change the subject.

Once again they were talking about Lyn and the Marquis's other possessions.

When finally they left the Restaurant, the carriage was waiting outside and Vilma found that the hood had been opened.

"You will be warm enough?" the Marquis asked.

"Yes, of course," she agreed, "it is a very warm night."

The Marquis did not miss the excitement in her eyes as the horses drove off.

They soon reached the road running along the Seine.

By now the stars had come out and were reflected in the water, as were the lights on the bridges.

Watching Vilma, the Marquis thought with amusement that she seemed again to have forgotten his presence.

She was so enthralled at what she was seeing that

she did not even trouble to talk to him.

He was used to women who, when driving with him in his carriage, moved nearer and nearer to him.

They would then slip a hand into his and raise their face invitingly.

But Vilma's eyes were on the river, the lights, and the stars.

The Marquis told himself this was a new experience, which was extremely good for his ego.

They drove on.

When they reached the *Place de la Concorde,* the Marquis told the coachman to stop so that Vilma could see the fountains.

They were throwing their water into the air, iridescent as a rainbow as it fell back into the basin below.

The great height of the obelisk, which came from the ruins of Luxor, the statues by Gabriel, and the trees made a picture of beauty and mystery.

Neither the Marquis nor Vilma spoke until finally she said in a rapt little voice:

"It is so lovely . . . so perfectly lovely! I feel it cannot be real!"

"That is what I have been thinking about you!" the Marquis replied.

For a moment he thought she had not heard him.

Then she turned to look up at him, and the stars seemed to have fallen into her eyes.

"If I could be a part of this," she said, "then I would never ask for anything more of life than to live in a fairy-tale for ever!"

"I think you will do that anyway," the Marquis answered.

He signalled the coachman to move on, and they

drove twice round the *Place de la Concorde* before going up the *Champs-Élysées*.

At the top, they reached the *Arc de Triomphe,* which the Marquis explained to her had been commissioned by Napoleon Bonaparte, but not inaugurated until thirty years later in the reign of Louis Philippe.

Only as the horses turned to go back did Vilma murmur:

"Now I have seen . . . Paris!"

"Not all of it," the Marquis answered. "There is a great deal more I want to show you."

"And I want to see it," she answered. "But I must not encroach on your time. I am sure you have many other things to do with people who are far more important than I am."

She was speaking as she really thought.

The Marquis was aware there was no mock-modesty in what she had said.

"I can think of nothing that would please me more than to show you Paris," he said. "Tomorrow morning I will take you driving in the *Bois,* which I think you will find amusing. After that we will plan what we will do in the afternoon and we will have a wide choice of different delights."

"Can you . . . really spare . . . the time?" she asked.

"I think I can manage it," he answered.

"Then it is the most exciting thing I can imagine. Oh, thank you . . . thank you once again! It is something I always seem to be . . . saying to . . . you."

The Marquis thought he had never known anyone to thank him with a sincerity that seemed to come from the heart.

If he had given Vilma a diamond necklace, she could not have been more grateful.

As they were driving down the *Champs-Élysées* he asked:

"Where are you staying?"

Vilma hesitated.

Then she said:

"At number twenty-five *Rue du Faubourg St. Honoré.*"

The Marquis raised his eye-brows.

"Surely that is the house of a friend of mine."

"The *Vicomte* is not in residence," Vilma said quickly.

"And you and your Father are improving the electricity of the house," the Marquis remarked.

Vilma did not contradict him.

She thought she had managed very skilfully not to make him think that she and her Father were guests of the *Vicomte*.

"Then at least I know where to call for you tomorrow morning," the Marquis remarked as they drew near to the house. "Shall we say eleven-thirty? Or is that too early for you?"

Vilma laughed.

"I am always awake early. In fact, I like to ride before breakfast."

"So do I," the Marquis answered. "Perhaps it is something we shall be able to do together one day in England."

He thought as he spoke that it was very unlikely.

He could imagine what a lot of gossip there would be if he invited Vilma to Lyn and rode with her—before she started work on his chandeliers.

Vilma was, in fact, thinking that she would like to invite the Marquis to her home.

She did not think her Father's horses would be as good as the Marquis's.

At the same time, there were one or two on which he would look magnificent.

There were also a number of jumps he would find a challenge.

Then she told herself that once she and her Father had left Paris, she would never see the Marquis again.

She remembered now she had read about him in the Court Circulars.

He was a guest at parties to which her Father and Mother were not invited.

They were of course those which were patronised by The Prince of Wales.

The guests included a great number of the Beauties with whom he was constantly associated.

The Balls to which Vilma had been invited, and they were not yet many, were given by the Dowagers of the aristocracy.

They were mostly for their granddaughters, who were her contemporaries.

She could understand that what was called the "Smart Set" would think these intensely boring.

She only read of their entertainments in the newspapers.

It was unlikely she would ever attend Balls given by the Countess of Warwick.

Least of all was she likely to receive an invitation to Marlborough House.

"I shall never see the Marquis after I return to England," she told herself.

She therefore said aloud:

"If you are quite certain it will not bore you, I would love to drive with you in the *Bois* tomorrow."

"Then that is what I shall look forward to," the Marquis answered.

They were nearing the *Vicomte*'s house.

It suddenly struck the Marquis that if he was with any other woman, he would undoubtedly kiss her good-night.

He thought that if he kissed Vilma, her lips would be very soft, sweet, and innocent.

From what she had said, he was sure she had never been kissed.

He thought it would be exciting to be the first man to do so.

Then he knew she had been so frightened by the *Comte,* that if he touched her, it would upset her all the more.

She might disappear and he would never see her again.

That would be a penalty he had no wish to suffer.

He knew, as the horses came to a standstill, that he had enjoyed the evening.

Not for a moment had he been bored while they were driving or dining.

It was only now he realised he had not given a thought to the Princess or the darkness of the future ahead.

"Youth has an allurement all of its own," he had heard an old man say once.

He knew that what Vilma had shown him was the "allurement of youth."

It had been as exciting and pure as the beauty of the stars over the *Place de la Concorde* very different from the amusement Lisette had given him last night.

The carriage came to a standstill and the Marquis stepped out first.

As he held Vilma's hand in his to help her to alight,

he knew that he really wanted to see her again.

He had no intention of letting her escape him.

The footman had rung the bell, and a sleepy servant opened the door.

"Good-night, Vilma," the Marquis said.

"Good-night, My Lord," she replied, "and thank you once again for a wonderful, wonderful evening. It is something I shall always remember."

"The fairy-story has not yet ended," the Marquis smiled. "I will be here at eleven-thirty tomorrow."

He knew, by the light in her eyes as she looked up at him, that it was what she wanted to hear.

Then she walked in through the front-door and the Marquis got back into the carriage.

As he drove away, she stood waving to him, the light behind her haloing her fair hair.

He was thinking that she made a very lovely picture.

It was one he would like to hang in his Gallery.

* * *

Vilma walked into the hall and thanked the footman before she went upstairs.

As she reached the landing, she saw Herbert coming from her Father's room.

"Is Papa awake?" she asked.

He shook his head.

"Sleepin' like a new-born babe," he said. "That Doctor Blanc's a miracle worker with 'is 'ands."

"I am sure Papa will feel better tomorrow," Vilma said.

"Did ye 'ave a good time wi' your friends, Miss Vilma?" Herbert asked.

Because he had known her since a child, Vilma knew he was genuinely interested.

"I had a wonderful time . . . simply wonderful!" she replied. "Tomorrow morning I am going driving in the *Bois*, but it would be best if you did not mention it to Papa, because he worries about me."

" 'Is Lordship'll only be worryin' in case 'is friends find out 'e ain't so steady in th' saddle as 'e thinks hisself t' be," Herbert replied.

It was the sort of remark that only Herbert could make without it being impertinent or disloyal.

Vilma laughed.

"We must make sure that Papa does not lose his pride," she said, "and do not forget that no-one must know who we really are."

Herbert sniffed.

"All this play-actin'! It be a lot o' foolishness, if ye ask me!"

Vilma went to her own room.

She had told Marie not to wait up for her, and she undid her own gown.

Only when she looked in the mirror, as she brushed her long hair, did she ask herself if she had been insulted.

The Marquis had not thought for one moment that she was anything but the daughter of an Electrician.

He had assumed she was working with her Father and being paid for it.

She had, of course, been glad he had been deceived so that he did not ask awkward questions.

At the same time, it was humiliating.

She belonged to one of the oldest families in Debrett's Peerage. Yet it was not obvious to the Marquis that she was a Lady.

Herbert had referred to it as "play-acting," and that was what it was.

She thought it would have been nice if the Marquis had said that it was impossible to think of her doing anything that was menial.

He had simply accepted what she had told him.

He had thought the reason why she did not wish to meet the smart people in the Ritz was that she would feel inferior.

"How dare he think like that?" she asked herself.

On the other hand, if he had thought of her as a Lady, he would not have taken her out to dinner alone.

Nor would he have taken her for that enchanting drive under the stars.

'I suppose one has to pay for everything in life, one way or another,' Vilma thought philosophically, 'and it is obvious that while I am very impressed with the Marquis, he is not so impressed with me."

He had indeed paid her some compliments.

But now she wondered if he really meant them.

She had the uncomfortable feeling that he looked on her only as a child to whom it amused him to be kind, not, as she had been in London, as an outstanding *débutante*.

Then she had to admit to herself that, for an "outstanding *débutante*," she had behaved in an extremely reprehensible manner, especially with anyone as well known and distinguished as the Marquis.

'It obviously would have been much less fun if he had invited two more people to join us,' she thought, 'but I just wish that he had indicated that he thought me more important than merely an Electrician's daughter.'

She pulled back the curtains and looked up at the stars.

Once again she had that exciting feeling that was almost an ecstasy.

It was what she had felt when she looked at the beauty of the fountains in the *Place de la Concorde.*

When they said good night, the Marquis had promised that the fairy-tale was not yet finished.

'I shall see him tomorrow,' Vilma consoled herself.

As she got into bed, she told herself that nothing else was of any consequence.

chapter five

PIERRE Blanc called to see the Earl at eleven o'clock.

At half-past the Marquis arrived.

Vilma knew she was quite safe in going out, as her Father would not want her then.

He would fall asleep as soon as *Monsieur* Blanc left him.

It was a lovely day, the sun shining out of a blue sky.

Vilma chose the prettiest of her hats to wear with one of her most elegant gowns.

She thought, although she was not certain, that the Marquis looked at her approvingly as she came out of the front-door.

He was waiting, with a Chaise even smarter than the one in which he had driven Lisette the previous morning, drawn by an even finer pair of horses.

The groom, who sat in the small seat behind, helped Vilma into the Chaise.

"Good-morning, Vilma," the Marquis said. "I hope you slept well?"

"I dreamt of the *Place de la Concorde,"* she answered, "and also of the *Arc de Triomphe."*

The Marquis smiled.

He knew that most women would have said they had dreamt of him.

He had learnt to accept that, as far as Vilma was concerned, he took second place to the beauty of Paris.

As they drove towards the *Bois,* Vilma said:

"It is very exciting to be driving with you, and I am sure you drive better than any Frenchman could."

"That is a compliment I appreciate," the Marquis said, "and I hope that is what I do."

When they reached the *Bois,* Vilma found that the Marquis had quite a lot of competition.

There were a number of Frenchmen in very new model Chaises, driving at tremendous speeds.

Others were going slowly so that they could talk to their friends who were on foot.

When Vilma saw the *cocottes* in their fantastic carriages, her eyes widened.

The Marquis knew she was astonished.

She did not say anything, however, until she saw a very attractive woman in an open carriage surrounded by a number of men, all very smartly dressed.

"Who is that?" Vilma asked.

"That is 'La Belle Otero,' " the Marquis replied.

"My Father said I should not speak of her," Vilma said without thinking.

"Why did he say that?" the Marquis enquired.

"He said that neither my Grandmother nor my Mother would ever mention her by name," Vilma replied ingenuously.

The Marquis smiled.

As they passed the carriage, La Belle Otero waved to him, and he swept off his hat.

"Do you know her?" Vilma asked as they drove on.

"She is appearing at the *Folies Bergères*," the Marquis replied, "and is an outstanding dancer."

"Oh, I would love to see her!" Vilma exclaimed.

The Marquis smiled again.

"I think your Father would disapprove of your going to the *Folies Bergères*."

"Why should he do that?" Vilma enquired.

The Marquis was silent as he drove on. Then he said:

"The *Folies Bergères* is unique to Paris. It has now become a Revue and is one of the most talked-of places in the whole of the Variety World."

Vilma thought it sounded fascinating.

"And La Belle Otero dances there?"

"She dances and very beautifully."

"Then why is it wrong for me to talk about her?" Vilma asked.

The Marquis thought he could explain that quite simply, but it would be a mistake.

He had never before met a woman with whom he could discuss so many subjects impersonally, just as he could with a man.

However, although Vilma was very intelligent, he was aware that in regard to love and sex, she was completely innocent.

She glanced at him as he did not reply, and after a minute she said:

"I suppose I ought not to ask you questions like that, but when I am with Papa we talk about anything that comes up. I forget there are certain subjects on which I should remain silent."

"I hope I come into the same category as your Father," the Marquis remarked, "and that we can discuss anything without feeling embarrassed."

"Even La Belle Otero?" Vilma asked.

"I think she is talked about quite enough without you and me adding to it," the Marquis said dryly. "Suppose instead I tell you about Kara Leonce, who has made a great name for herself by hanging by her teeth from a flying trapeze?"

This made Vilma laugh so much that La Belle Otero was forgotten.

The Marquis, however, was wondering what she would think of the new mode for immodesty.

The Paris Art students had, a few years ago, rented the Moulin Rouge for their celebrated "Four Arts Ball."

During the evening two of the girls compared legs and others quickly joined in the competition.

Suddenly one of the models, very proud of her charms, jumped on a table, confident of victory.

Mona, as she was called, meant no harm.

But, after she had stripped naked, the Police called on her next morning.

She was taken before the Magistrates with several other girls who had followed her example.

They were all fined a hundred *francs* and given time to pay.

The sentence was a light one, but it was too much for the Latin Quarter, and two days later a revolt began.

The result was to make headlines in the newspapers all over the world.

A year later, because a woman entirely naked was to be seen there, a poky little Music Hall in the *Rue des Martyrs* was turning crowds away every night.

That was the beginning.

Although the *Folies Bergères* did not go quite so far, performers there certainly displayed a great deal of bare flesh.

It would be a mistake, the Marquis decided, for him to take Vilma to the *Folies Bergères*.

Nevertheless, he thought it would be interesting to watch her reaction.

They drove in the crowded, then in the quieter parts of the *Bois*.

Then the Marquis took Vilma to luncheon at a Restaurant by the Seine.

It was high up on the Third Floor.

Sitting near a window, Vilma could watch the barges moving up and down the river.

She could see the gulls that had flown inland from the sea, and the sunshine shimmering on the moving water.

She was thrilled by everything, just as the Marquis had expected she would be.

He was aware that none of the other women he had brought to this particular Restaurant had looked out of the window.

They had kept their eyes fixed on him.

"I am sure Paris is the most beautiful City in the world," Vilma said as she turned her head to concentrate on her plate. "And also the food is more delicious than anything I have ever eaten before."

"I always think the same when I come to Paris," the Marquis said, "and although my Chef is exceedingly good, the French have a knack of making every dish they offer you a work of art."

"That is just the right description," Vilma exclaimed,

"and I shall remember you said that when I go back to England."

"Is that the only thing you will remember about me?" the Marquis enquired.

"No, of course not!" Vilma replied. "It has been wonderful being with you and talking about all the things that interest me, but which never seem to interest other women."

The Marquis smiled at her.

"Most of them, I think," he said, "are preoccupied with love, and that is something about which I feel you know very little."

"I have never been in love," Vilma admitted, "but I think it must be a very . . . marvellous feeling, like touching the stars, or climbing up to the moon."

"Some people think of it as the burning heart of the sun," the Marquis said.

Vilma was quiet for a moment. Then she replied:

"I do not quite understand. What do you mean?"

"When you marry," the Marquis replied, "your husband will teach you. It is something which is difficult to put into words, but which you will feel with your heart."

"And of course . . . my soul," Vilma added quickly. "I know that love is . . . part of the soul."

The Marquis thought she always had something original to say, and of course she was right, although he doubted if his soul had ever been engaged in any of his many love-affairs with beautiful women.

They finished luncheon, and as the Marquis and Vilma left the Restaurant, he said:

"I am going to take you home, but first we will drive and look at the Eiffel Tower and perhaps tomorrow you would like to climb to the top of it?"

"I would love that," Vilma agreed. "But are you quite certain you can spare the time to be with me again tomorrow?"

"I think I can manage it," the Marquis replied as he had before.

Vilma gave a cry of delight before she said:

"When I said my prayers last night I found it difficult to say 'thank you' enough to God for bringing you into my life. I should have found it very dreary while Papa is asleep just to go shopping with one of the house-maids, and I should never have known where to go if it had not been for you."

"We have not yet done the Louvre," the Marquis said, "but I am keeping that for a rainy day."

"Supposing we do not have one?"

"Then of course we shall have to force ourselves out of the sunshine simply because the Louvre will be good for our education."

The way he said it made Vilma laugh.

As they drove towards the Eiffel Tower, she found herself laughing at so many of the things the Marquis told her.

She was delighted to find that she could make him laugh too.

It was nearly four o'clock when they turned towards the *Rue St. Honoré*.

"I have a special place for us to dine tonight," the Marquis said. "You will find that the food is superb and the Restaurant is exactly as it was before the Revolution."

"Are you really . . . inviting me to . . . dine with you . . . again?" Vilma asked.

"You can hardly leave me to dine alone with no-one to make me laugh," the Marquis protested.

"I cannot imagine why you are so kind to me," Vilma said. "I am not so foolish as not to be aware that there are many beautiful Ladies staying at the Ritz Hotel who would love to dine with you."

"They will have to manage without me," the Marquis said, "and of course I must look after you."

That morning, when they had passed La Belle Otero in the *Bois,* he had seen that among the men leaning over her carriage was the *Comte* Gaston de Forêt.

Vilma had not noticed him.

The Marquis, however, was aware that the *Comte* had stiffened when he saw to whom La Belle Otero was waving.

He had stared penetratingly at Vilma.

Because the Marquis knew she was still frightened of the *Comte,* he had whipped up his horses.

He was relieved that Vilma had been unaware of the *Comte*'s presence.

He had, therefore, continued their drive in the *Bois* before luncheon without mentioning him.

Now, on reaching the *Rue St. Honoré,* he drew up his Chaise outside the *Vicomte*'s house.

Vilma had been looking in her hand-bag.

As he brought the horses to a standstill, she said a little shyly:

"I . . . I wrote a note to thank . . . you for all your kindness and hospitality to . . . me yesterday. There seems no point in posting it to the Ritz when I can . . . see you . . . so here it . . . is."

"Your first *billet-doux,"* the Marquis remarked without thinking.

He realised that he had made Vilma blush, before she said hastily:

"It is . . . very inadequate in saying what I . . . want to say."

The groom had jumped down to help her alight.

She walked up the steps, then turned to wave to the Marquis.

He raised his hat as he drove off, tooling his horses carefully through the crowded traffic back to the *Place Vendôme*.

He drew up outside the Ritz Hotel.

The groom came to the side of the Chaise to take the reins from him.

The Marquis handed them to him, saying as he did so:

"Thank your Master for sending me these horses, and tell him I found them easy to handle and an outstanding pair."

"He'll be pleased to know that, *M'sieur*," the groom said, "but they can't compare with th' chestnuts owned by th' *Comte* de Forêt."

"Where did you see those?" the Marquis asked.

"Outside the house you've just left, *M'sieur*," the groom replied. "I didn't think you'd miss 'em."

The Marquis stared at him.

"Outside the *Vicomte*'s house?" he enquired as if the groom must be mistaken.

"That's right, *M'sieur*. I knows 'is coachman, an' 'e tells me *M'sieur le Comte* only bought th' chestnuts a month ago."

The Marquis grabbed the reins back from the groom's hand.

"Get in!" he said curtly.

Turning the horses, he drove back the way he had come, going a great deal faster than he had before.

It took him only a short while to reach the *Vicomte*'s house.

He saw that the groom had not misled him.

Outside, drawn to one side so that they were in the shade of a tree, stood a superb pair of chestnuts.

He noted that the coachman sitting on the box was wearing the *Comte* de Forêt's livery.

The Marquis did not wait for his groom to alight.

He jumped from the Chaise and pulled at the bell violently.

At the same time, he raised the knocker of the door.

It was opened by a man-servant.

At the Marquis walked into the Hall, he heard Vilma scream.

* * *

Vilma had left the Marquis feeling as if she were living in the fairy-tale of which they had spoken.

The whole time they had spent together had been enchanted.

The *Bois,* with its elegantly-dressed women, the fine horses, and smart riders, might have been part of a play on the stage of Drury Lane.

There was nothing to be compared with the beauty of the Seine, she'd thought while they had luncheon.

Nor the excitement of seeing the Eiffel Tower as it rose high above them.

She had enjoyed listening as the Marquis described what had happened at the opening of it, at which he had been present.

"I shall see him again tonight," she told herself as he drove away.

She went into the Hall and the servant shut the door behind her.

"There's a Gentleman waiting t' see you, *M'mselle,*" he said.

"A Gentleman?" Vilma queried.

She thought it must be either the Doctor or else *Monsieur* Blanc, who had wanted to tell her how the treatment was progressing.

Without thinking, she took off her hat with its elegant feathers and put it down on a chair.

The man-servant opened the door of the Drawing-Room for her.

As she entered the room, patting her hair into place at the sides, she was wondering what news she would have of her Father.

There was a man at the far end of the Drawing-Room, which was quite large, standing with his back to her.

She was half-way down the room before she realised that it was neither the Doctor nor Pierre Blanc.

At her approach, he turned and she saw with horror that it was the *Comte* de Forêt.

She stopped dead, thinking he looked even more unpleasant than she remembered.

She also felt afraid because they were alone.

"Good-afternoon, my beautiful Angel!" the *Comte* said.

"Why . . . why are . . . you here?" Vilma asked. "How . . . did you . . . find me?"

"It took a great deal of detective work on my part," the *Comte* replied, "but of course, I had to return something you left behind in my bedroom."

He held up, as he spoke, Vilma's gloves.

She had, in fact, forgotten all about them.

She remembered, too late, that when the Marquis had retrieved her hat she had not asked him to bring back her gloves also.

Now the *Comte* had found her.

As if she asked the question again, he said:

"César Ritz was most discreet and told me he had no idea where you were staying, which I suspected to be a lie."

"Then, how . . ." Vilma began.

"The Electrician whom you were helping with my chandelier," the *Comte* interrupted, "was considerably more helpful. He told me where the chandelier had come from, and of course the *Vicomte* is an old friend of mine."

"Thank you for bringing back my . . . gloves," Vilma managed to say, "and now, if you will excuse me . . . I wish to go . . . upstairs and see . . . my Father."

"Not so fast!" the *Comte* said. "It may surprise you, my beautiful Angel, to know that I have been unable to stop thinking about you ever since I found you in my bedroom. In fact, I have dreamt of you!"

"I find that hard to believe, *Monsieur*."

"Then I must try to convince you," the *Comte* said. "So I suggest we sit down and you make yourself pleasant to me."

He glanced around the room before he added:

"I see you have made yourself comfortable in the *Vicomte*'s absence!"

Vilma stiffened.

She realised that, like the Marquis, he had assumed that she was a professional Electrician.

The *Comte* was therefore making it clear she was imposing on the *Vicomte* by using his best rooms when he was away from home.

She thought it exceedingly rude of him.

"I think, *Monsieur,*" she said, "that you are being insulting. I can only ask you to leave me alone because I have other things to attend to."

"I cannot believe they are more important than me," the *Comte* answered, "and there are many things I want to talk to you about, which I think will be to your advantage."

"I can think of nothing more important at the moment than that I should have a rest," Vilma retorted.

She was wondering desperately how she could get rid of him.

She was aware that her Father would be asleep upstairs.

The servants were not likely to interrupt them.

Anyway, they would be nervous of trying to persuade the *Comte* to leave, if he refused to do so.

"I must somehow make him go," Vilma told herself, "but I want to avoid having a scene."

With an effort she managed to say in a more pleasant tone of voice:

"It is very kind of you, *Monsieur,* to bring me back my gloves, but I am sure you will understand that I am tired after a long drive, and I really do need to rest."

"Suppose I rest with you?" the *Comte* asked. "I cannot believe that you would deny me the comfort that you are according yourself."

Vilma thought that he was teasing her and making a joke which she did not think was very funny.

She walked to the mantelpiece.

She put her gloves down on a table which was on one side of it.

She was vividly aware as she did so that the *Comte* was watching her.

There was the same expression in his dark eyes which had frightened her before.

"You are lovely—exquisite!" he said. "From the first moment I saw you above me in the sky, I wanted you to be mine."

"You frightened me," Vilma replied. "I was very grateful to the Marquis for helping me to escape from you."

"Curse him! He is always interfering in my life!" the *Comte* exclaimed.

They were speaking in French and the *Comte* used a coarse swear-word.

Vilma was aware he would not have done so with anyone he believed to be a Lady of Quality.

She did not reply, and the *Comte* went on:

"Listen to me attentively. I want you to be mine and I will make it very worthwhile. In fact, you will not have to work for your living ever again. Is that clear?"

Vilma just stared at him.

She could not understand for the moment what he was saying.

And yet, instinctively, she knew it was an insult.

While she was hesitating in finding the words with which to reply, the *Comte* came closer to her.

"You cannot run away from me," he said, "and I am going to take you in my arms as I wanted to do the first moment I saw you."

With a swiftness that took him by surprise, Vilma moved away from him.

She wanted to reach the door, but he was standing directly in front of it.

She therefore moved sideways so that she was near to the window.

"Go away!" she demanded. "Leave me alone! I do not understand what you are saying to me, but I am quite sure you are insulting me."

"Do you really think I would insult you," the *Comte* asked, "when all I want is to kiss you? I promise you that you will find it very exciting and will no longer try to run away from me."

"But that is what I intend to do," Vilma declared firmly.

As she spoke, she made a movement towards the door, but he was too quick for her.

He stood directly in her way and flung out his arms.

She knew by the expression on his face and the sudden alertness she could see in his eyes, that he was actually enjoying the fact that she was fighting him.

He wanted to make her surrender—to conquer her.

She was so vividly aware of it that the terror she had felt when he first touched her suddenly swept over her again.

Now it was even more frightening than it had been before because the door was closed.

She felt sure that no-one would hear her if she cried out for help.

She wondered if she could plead with him.

"Please . . . please . . . *Monsieur* . . ." she began.

Her voice was almost incoherent and she trembled.

The *Comte* was coming nearer and nearer, but slowly, as if he were savouring the delay.

At the same time, she knew he wanted to intimidate her.

"You are mine!" he muttered, and it was the snarl of an animal.

Desperately she tried to escape, but it was too late.

He caught hold of her, pulling her roughly against him, and she screamed.

Then he was holding her tightly against his chest.

His lips were seeking hers, but were prevented from touching them only because she kept turning her head desperately from side to side.

She was so frightened that she felt as if the whole world had gone dark.

The *Comte*'s arms were like bars of steel.

She had the terrifying feeling that it was only a question of seconds before she would be completely in his power.

It was then, when he held her so closely that she could hardly breathe, that she heard an English voice say:

"What the hell is going on here?"

It was the Marquis, and Vilma knew she was saved for the second time.

The *Comte* was still holding her, but the Marquis caught hold of him from behind and pulled him away.

Then, with a violent blow with his clenched fist, the Marquis knocked him to the ground and the *Comte* released his hold on Vilma.

Vilma staggered, but managed to remain on her feet.

She put out her hands blindly towards the Marquis as the *Comte* raised himself.

"You struck me, Lynworth," he said, "and, by God, you shall pay for it!"

"Somebody has to stop you from behaving like a reptile!" the Marquis replied coolly.

With an effort, the *Comte* rose from the ground.

"I demand satisfaction!" he said. "Or are you too much of a coward to accept my challenge?"

"I will fight you anywhere you wish," the Marquis said calmly. "You have only to name the place, and I will teach you a lesson you will never forget."

The *Comte* pulled his coat back into place.

"Very well," he said, "and do not blame me, My Lord, if you suffer and, I hope, acutely!"

"I am waiting for you to tell me where we shall meet," the Marquis said. "I presume it will be the *Bois* at some unearthly hour tomorrow morning."

"On the contrary," the *Comte* snarled, "you will meet me tonight at eleven o'clock in my garden, which is lit by electricity, of which this capricious young woman knows so much."

"You can leave her out of our conversation," the Marquis warned him.

"Considering that she is the prize over which we are fighting, that is impossible!" the *Comte* asserted. "Moreover, I insist on her being present at the duel in which you will meet your Master!"

The Marquis did not reply, and the *Comte* said in his most unpleasant tone:

"I shall expect you at eleven o'clock, unless, of course you 'chicken out'!"

"You can count on my presence," the Marquis said, "and I presume you will provide a Referee."

"Naturally," the *Comte* agreed.

He walked towards the door.

Then he turned and looked back to say to Vilma:

"*Au revoir,* my lovely Angel. After tonight there will be no-one to thwart me and you will be mine, as I always intended."

He walked out of the Drawing-Room, slamming the door behind him.

Only when he had gone did Vilma give a cry of horror as she flung herself against the Marquis.

"You must . . . not . . . fight him . . . you must . . . not!" she cried. "He is evil and . . . wicked and he . . . intends to . . . injure you! Please . . . please . . . do not . . . fight him . . . on my . . . account!"

She was holding on to him and looking up, while the intensity of her feelings brought tears to her eyes.

Very slowly the Marquis put his arms around her.

"Do you really think I would let a swine like that win you for himself?"

The way he spoke was different from the way he had ever spoken to her before.

Vilma looked up at him enquiringly.

As she did so, he drew her closer and his lips came down on hers.

He kissed her gently, knowing it was the first time she had been kissed.

Her lips were trembling.

At the same time, he found, as he had expected, that they were soft, sweet, and innocent.

He felt a quiver run through Vilma, and without being aware of it she pressed herself a little closer to him.

Now his lips became more demanding, more passionate, and more possessive.

To Vilma it was as if the sky had opened and a Divine Light enveloped them both.

She had been so shocked, so appalled as the *Comte* snarled at the Marquis, that all she could think of was him.

She was afraid from the way the *Comte* was speaking that he intended to injure the Marquis seriously.

Now, as the wonder of his kiss swept over her, she knew that she loved him.

It was love that was seeping through her, running through her veins.

It gave her an ecstasy beyond anything she had ever dreamt of feeling.

It was part of the beauty of the Seine, the stars, the *Place de la Concorde,* and the wonder of being with the Marquis.

It was so much more even than that, she could not describe it.

It seemed to throb in her heart or, as she had said herself, her soul.

Only when the Marquis raised his head did she manage to say, with a lilt in her voice like the song of a bird:

"I love you . . . I love you . . . I did not . . . know that . . . love was like . . . this!"

"And I love you," the Marquis said, "but I was afraid to tell you so in case I frightened you, my lovely one."

"You do . . . love me? You really . . . love me?"

"I am being entirely truthful," the Marquis said, "when I tell you that I have never felt like this about anybody before."

He kissed her again because he had no words with which to express his feelings.

She knew that what he was saying was part of the mystery of which he had spoken.

In fact, it was the "burning heart of the sun."

Only when the room seemed to be swinging dizzily round her did the Marquis move her to the sofa.

They sat down with his arms around her.

"How can you be so absurdly beautiful?" he asked. "And so different that there are no words with which to describe you?"

Vilma put her head against his shoulder.

"I did not . . . know that . . . love could be so . . . wonderful," she whispered.

"I will teach you about love, my Darling," the Marquis said, "and it will be the most exciting thing I have ever done in my life."

He felt her quiver before she said quickly:

"You must . . . not fight that . . . terrible man! I know he intends to . . . maim you . . . perhaps even . . . kill you!"

"It is a matter of honour, my Precious," the Marquis replied, "and I must therefore accept his challenge."

He kissed her forehead before he went on:

"I can assure you I am not afraid of a bounder like that! If he has his arm in a sling for the next two months, it will be his own fault!"

Vilma looked up at him.

"Please . . . please . . . let us . . . run away and . . . forget about him," she begged.

"I long to run away with you," the Marquis said, "but first I have to behave like a Gentleman, and at the same time teach that swine a lesson he will never forget!"

"But . . . please . . ." Vilma began.

The Marquis held her lips captive, and she was unable to say what she wanted.

Because he was kissing her, she could think of nothing else.

There was only the song of the Angels, the light of Heaven, and an ecstasy that carried them both up into the sky.

chapter six

A LONG time later the Marquis said:

"I must change, Darling, and take you out to dinner. I think we both deserve a good meal."

Vilma gave a little shiver.

She could not help thinking it might be the last time they would ever be together.

The Marquis kissed her again.

Finally, he rose from the sofa and she made no protest.

She only thought how handsome he was and how much she loved him.

He walked to the door. Then he said:

"I will come back for you at nine o'clock and I shall be counting the minutes, my Precious, until I can kiss you again."

He saw her eyes shining as if they had caught the sunshine.

With an effort he walked out of the Drawing-Room, closing the door behind him.

Vilma put her hands over her face.

Was it possible? Could it really be true that the Marquis loved her as she loved him?

It had all seemed to happen so swiftly.

She could hardly believe she was not dreaming it all and would wake up to find herself not in Paris, but in London.

She went upstairs to see her Father, but she did not want to tell him yet what had happened.

She knew he had always admired the Marquis's horses.

She felt, therefore, that he would be pleased that she had found a man she really loved and who loved her.

Yet, for the moment, she could not speak of it to anyone.

It was too precious, like a living throbbing jewel in her breast.

Herbert was waiting outside her Father's room.

"You're too late, Miss," he announced. " 'Is Lordship . . . I means the Colonel's been waitin' for you, but now 'e's fallen asleep. It'd be a shame to disturb 'im when 'e's better'n 'e's ever bin."

"I am so glad about that," Vilma said, "and of course I will not disturb Papa if he is asleep."

"That's wot that Doctor said 'e's got t'do," Herbert said, "an' when th' treatment's over 'e passes out like a light!"

Vilma smiled before she went to her own room.

She opened the wardrobe, and stood looking at her gowns.

Which one was beautiful enough for what she felt was the most marvellous night of her life?

Then she remembered what was to happen at eleven o'clock.

Instantly the fear was back again.

She dropped down on her knees beside her bed.

She prayed fervently that the Marquis would not be hurt.

She knew very little about duels except that in England they had been banned from taking place by Queen Victoria.

It was, however, whispered that they continued to take place surreptitiously.

Sometimes one of the duellists would be badly wounded.

"Please . . . oh . . . please . . . God," Vilma prayed, "let it be the *Comte* and . . . not the Marquis who is . . . injured."

She prayed until there was a knock on the door, and she knew it was Marie, come to help her dress.

"Chef wants to know, *M'mselle,* if you'll be in to dinner," Marie said.

"No, I am going out," Vilma replied. "But if my Father is having his meal at eight o'clock, I will sit with him."

"I thinks it's at half-past," Marie told her.

"Then I will sit with him," Vilma decided.

With a great deal of trouble Marie arranged a bath for Vilma.

A footman carried up the cans of hot water and the bath was arranged in front of the fireplace, although there was no fire.

Vilma soaked for some time in the scented water.

As there was no hurry, afterwards, she dressed slowly.

She took a great deal of trouble over her hair and

finally chose the gown she liked the best.

It was very elaborate, being one that had been bought for the more important Balls she was to attend in London.

However, having come abroad with her Father, she had missed several of them.

As Marie got her ready, Vilma was thinking how much she would like to dance with the Marquis.

She wanted more than anything else to be in his arms again and for him to kiss her.

"I love him! I love him!" she said to her reflection in the mirror.

When she went into her Father's bedroom, he was no longer asleep.

He did not, however, notice that she was more elaborately dressed than usual.

Nor did he ask her where she was going to dine.

He merely said he felt better, but was very tired.

"But my back no longer hurts me—which is all that matters!" he said.

"Oh, Papa, I am so glad!" Vilma exclaimed. "You will be riding again soon."

"I will break in that horse if it kills me!" the Earl murmured.

"I am sure *Monsieur* Blanc will not want you to ride anything obstreperous to start with . . ." Vilma began.

Then she realised her Father was not listening.

She was sure, whatever she said, he would do exactly what he wanted to do.

He was almost asleep before he had finished his dinner.

She kissed him affectionately.

In a way, she wished she could tell him what was

going to happen later to-night.

Then she was afraid he would forbid her to be present at a duel.

She knew it was something that would never happen to her in London.

People there would be very shocked if they knew she was a witness at a duel between two men which concerned herself.

She thought, however, that no-one in Paris would realise she was concerned.

What is more, both the *Comte* and the Marquis knew her only under her assumed name.

"And also as an Electrician!" she added to herself with a smile.

She was sure it would please the Marquis when she told him of her real identity.

"He loves me for myself, and that is something which I was always afraid might never happen."

She had been aware in London that the Dowagers pointed her out to their sons as being the daughter of an Earl who was very wealthy.

She had been too astute at even her first Ball not to realise this.

Some of the beardless young men danced with her not because she was pretty, but because she was Lady Vilma Dale.

"I will tell the Marquis who I really am after the duel is over," she decided.

It was difficult to wait patiently for nine o'clock.

Just as one of the clocks in the hall chimed the hour, she heard the sound of wheels outside the front-door.

She picked up her velvet wrap, which lay on a chair, and pulled it round her shoulders.

As the Marquis stepped into the Hall, she was waiting for him.

"I knew you would not keep me waiting." He smiled.

He took her hand in his, led her down the steps, and helped her into the closed carriage.

As the horses drove off, he put his arms around her.

"It seems like a century since I kissed you," he said.

Then he was kissing her possessively, and the world vanished.

There was only him and the love she felt for him.

The *Grand Vefour* was even more attractive than she had expected it to be.

It was a small Restaurant in the *Palais Royal* which, as the Marquis had said, had been there before the Revolution.

There were exquisitely painted panels of flowers on the walls, and large windows.

There were also comfortable red sofas on which to sit.

Only a few other people were dining there besides themselves.

Vilma let the Marquis choose the meal and the champagne they were to drink.

Only when the waiter had left them did he put his hand over hers and say:

"At last we are alone, and there are a great many things I want to talk to you about, my Darling. But first let me tell you that you are even lovelier than when I left you a few hours ago."

The way he was looking at her made Vilma feel little thrills run through her body.

Her fingers quivered beneath his.

"How can you be lovelier than any woman I ever imagined existed?" the Marquis asked. "Sometimes I think I must have dreamt you."

"That is what . . . I felt . . . this evening," Vilma replied. "I was afraid I would wake up to find I was not in Paris, but in London and you were only a part of my dreams!"

"I am very, very real!" the Marquis assured her. "As I will prove to you later."

When the food arrived it was delicious, but Vilma was hardly aware of what she was eating.

All she was conscious of was the Marquis's grey eyes looking at her with love.

Everything he said to her seemed precious and something she wanted always to remember.

When dinner was over, coffee was served with a glass of brandy for the Marquis.

Then he said:

"I want to talk to you seriously, my lovely one."

Vilma looked up at him and he went on:

"Just in case something untoward happens tonight, I have made a Will which has been witnessed by César Ritz and my valet, leaving you a considerable sum of money."

Vilma gave a little cry.

"You are not to talk like . . . that! How can you . . . imagine, even for a moment . . . that you . . . might die?"

"We have to be sensible about this," the Marquis replied. "It is something that could happen, and if it does, I could not bear to think of you, my Darling, having to work for a living, or being in a position where you had to accept money from a man like the *Comte*."

Vilma stared at him, not understanding.

Then he said in a rather strange voice:

"I love you! You know I love you more than I have ever loved any woman in my whole life! But I cannot marry you!"

Vilma drew in her breath.

She had never thought, never imagined he would say anything like that.

"I want, more than I want anything the world can give me, to make you my wife," the Marquis continued, "and God knows I want you with me always and for ever—but it is impossible!"

Still Vilma did not speak.

She could only look at him, trying to take in what he was saying.

"I came to Paris," the Marquis went on, "because a marriage has been planned for me by my Mother to Princess Helgie of Whitenberg."

He paused before he said fiercely:

"I do not know her. I saw her once when she was a child, and I had no wish to marry her or anybody else—until I met you. But she has been invited to England, and I have been placed in a position where it is impossible not to ask her to be my wife."

There was a note of despair in the Marquis's voice.

Vilma could not speak.

She could only stare at him, thinking that what she was hearing could not be true.

There was a long pause.

Then in a voice he could hardly hear, and which seemed to come from a long way away, Vilma asked:

"Are you . . . telling me that . . . after tonight . . . I . . . I shall . . . never see you . . . again?"

"Of course I am not saying that," the Marquis replied

quickly. "What I am telling you is that I love you and want you to be part of my life. I cannot lose you."

He made a sound of exasperation before he went on:

"I want you unbearably, but it will not be possible for us to be together all the time."

He put out his hand to take hers before he said:

"I will arrange somehow to have you near me, whether we are in London or in the country."

He stopped to smile at her.

"There will be times when we can escape and come to Paris or anywhere else that takes our fancy. All I ask is that you trust me and love me as I love you."

Slowly Vilma began to understand what he was asking of her.

She felt as if the floor had opened beneath her feet to reveal a dark chasm into which she was falling.

She could feel a pain within her breast that was an agony.

Some part of her seemed to be frozen into numbness.

She felt that what she was hearing could not be true.

"We will be happy—I know we will be happy!" the Marquis said almost violently. "I will make sure, my lovely one, that you will never regret allowing me to look after you and protect you from being insulted by men like the *Comte*."

It flashed through Vilma's mind that what the Marquis was suggesting was very much the same as what the *Comte* had offered.

Her voice trembled as she asked:

"Are you really saying . . . that you . . . cannot marry me because . . . I am not . . . good enough for . . . you?"

"It is not that," the Marquis protested. "You are too good, too beautiful, too pure for any man. But in my position as head of the family it is obligatory that 'blue blood' goes to 'blue blood.' I cannot demean the family name which has been maintained and respected all through the centuries."

Vilma pressed her lips tightly together.

She thought that if she behaved properly she would get up from the sofa on which she was sitting and leave him.

If he had his pride, she had hers.

But she knew she could not do such a thing at this particular moment.

Not when he was about to fight a duel with the *Comte* on her behalf.

If she were to do something which upset him, he might shoot badly.

And if in consequence he died, it would be her fault.

"I must not answer . . . I must keep . . . silent," she told herself.

"We will talk about this tomorrow," the Marquis said. "Time is getting on now, and I have to pick up a friend who has agreed to act as one of my seconds."

As if Vilma has asked the question, he added:

"You will not know him and he will not know you. He has only just arrived from Rome, where he has been at our Embassy for over two years."

"He will not . . . talk about . . . what has . . . happened," Vilma managed to say.

The Marquis shook his head.

"Peter is discretion itself, thanks to his Diplomatic training, and also because we have always been close friends."

As the Marquis spoke, he signalled to the waiter to bring him the bill.

It was ready for him, and having settled it, he rose to his feet.

He put the velvet wrap round Vilma's shoulders.

They walked from the Restaurant the short distance to where the carriage was waiting for them.

As they drove off, Vilma felt the Marquis's arms go round her.

For the first time, she wanted to resist him.

She did not want him to kiss her.

He had betrayed the love she had given him.

She told herself that if the situation were reversed and he was of no more importance than a simple Clerk, it would have made no difference to her.

She would love him exactly the same as she did now.

Then her common sense told her that it could not have been exactly the same.

Her family would have fought with every weapon in their power to prevent her from marrying a man they considered socially beneath her.

Although the Marquis had not said so, she knew his family would do the same.

They had chosen a Royal Princess to be his bride.

Was it likely they would accept, however ardently he pleaded with them, the daughter of an Electrician who worked for César Ritz?

The Marquis drew her closer.

"You are not to be frightened, my Darling," he said, "nor are you to worry about me. I promise you I can look after myself, and when this unpleasantness is behind us, we will forget about it and be as ecstatically happy as we were this afternoon."

Vilma was so apprehensive about the duel, that for the time being she forgot her own feelings.

"You will . . . be careful . . . very, very careful?" she begged. "And you will . . . not take . . . any risks?"

"There is always some risk when one is fighting a duel," the Marquis replied. "At the same time, I flatter myself I am a good shot and, I am sure, a better one than de Forêt, who has led an extremely dissipated life."

Vilma hoped this was true.

At the same time, she knew the *Comte* would fight like a ferocious tiger, which the Marquis had once said he resembled.

"He hates . . . you!" she cried aloud. "And I am sure he intends to injure you."

"You are not to upset yourself," the Marquis said. "What happens is in the lap of the Gods, and of course I shall have your prayers, my Darling, to support me and to shield me from all evil."

"I will be praying . . . you know I will be praying," Vilma said. "At the same time, the *Comte* is evil . . . I can feel it . . . vibrating from him."

She would have said a great deal more, but the Marquis pulled her close to him and kissed her.

He released her only when the horses came to a standstill outside the Ritz.

"Peter is waiting here for me," the Marquis explained. "His name is Hampton and his Father is the Leader of the House of Lords."

As he finished speaking, the door was opened.

Before the Marquis could get out, a tall, very handsome young man climbed in.

"I was waiting for you, Vernon," he said, "because time is getting on."

"Well, we are here," the Marquis replied, "and let me introduce you to Vilma Crawshaw."

Peter Hampton sat down on the seat opposite them and put out his hand.

As Vilma took it, she knew he was sincere and, like the Marquis, someone she could trust.

"I told Peter," the Marquis was saying, "that, contrary to all the rules, you have been invited to the duel. In fact, my opponent has insisted on your presence."

"It is . . . better than sitting at home . . . wondering what is . . . happening," Vilma murmured.

"I agree with you," Peter Hampton said, "and I intend to keep a sharp eye on de Forêt. There have been some unpleasant tales about him. The last time he fought a duel his opponent lay between life and death for several months."

Vilma gave a cry of horror, and the Marquis said quickly:

"You are not to frighten Vilma! She is very upset already about the whole thing."

"I am not surprised," Peter Hampton said, "and I will do my best to take care of you."

He spoke with a touch of laughter in his voice, as if the Marquis were too big and strong to need somebody to cosset him.

In the darkness inside the carriage, Vilma slipped her hand into the Marquis's.

His fingers closed over hers.

The horses did not take long to reach the *Comte* de Forêt's house which was just off the *Champs-Élyseés*.

It was a fine-looking mansion, surrounded by trees.

As they turned in through the iron gates, Vilma could see there was a large garden.

She did not realise until she alighted that when Peter Hampton had joined them at the Ritz, another man had stepped up onto the box beside the coachman.

She thought he looked like a valet and was not surprised when the Marquis said:

"This is Barker, who has been with me since I was a boy and disapproves very strongly of duels."

"That's true, M'Lord," Barker agreed. "As I've said afore, 'tis a great mistake for Yer Lordship t' be takin' part in one."

He spoke, Vilma thought, like a disapproving Nanny.

The Marquis laughed and answered:

"Barker always anticipates the worst. If he had his way, I would be wrapped up in cotton-wool and put in a glass case!"

"Just the right place for you," Peter Hampton teased. "Now—where is our host?"

A servant speaking in rapid French asked them to follow him.

He did not take them into the house, but round the side of it.

At the back there were more trees and a number of flowering shrubs.

Surrounded by them, Vilma saw what she guessed was a Bowling-Green.

It was certainly, she thought, an excellent place for a duel.

The shrubs and trees prevented them from being overlooked even by anyone in the house.

At the far end she saw the *Comte* standing with three men.

Vilma knew as she followed the Marquis towards

him that his eyes were on her.

Her hatred for him rose within her.

She wished she could hurt him in some way and make him feel uncomfortable by what she said.

However, before they reached him, she and Peter Hampton stopped.

The Marquis went forward alone.

They stood watching him, with Barker a little way behind them.

It was then that the electric lights were turned on.

Vilma saw that the whole Bowling-Green was skilfully lit.

There were not any blazing lights that could dazzle anyone.

They were arranged so that the area of the Bowling-Green was as clear as daylight, surrounded by shadow.

Vilma saw Peter Hampton looking about with interest.

Having shaken hands with an elderly man who Vilma guessed was the Referee, the Marquis returned to them.

"They are eager to get this over as quickly as possible," he said, "and that suits me."

The *Comte* made no move to approach Vilma or Peter Hampton.

The Referee shook hands with them, then walked to the centre of the Bowling-Green.

There were two duelling pistols on the ground, and he invited the Marquis to choose which one he preferred.

He did not hurry over this, but examined the pistols carefully.

He finally gave one to Peter to hold while he took off his coat.

While he was doing so, the Referee invited Vilma to sit down on a chair.

It was just behind where he was standing.

"It is very unusual, *Mademoiselle,*" he said in a quiet voice, "for a Lady to be present at such proceedings."

"I know that," Vilma answered, "but I could not refuse, and if I am honest, did not wish to do so."

The Referee, who was a nice-looking man, smiled at her.

"It is a pity that we cannot meet in more pleasant circumstances," he said gallantly.

Vilma was watching the Marquis and Peter, who were talking together in low voices.

It was then she was aware when she looked at the end of the Bowling-Green they had just left that the *Comte* was wearing a black shirt.

Vaguely at the back of her mind, she seemed to have heard somebody say that duellists who lacked self-confidence took the precaution of wearing inconspicuous clothes.

It was obvious that the Marquis had no intention of dressing himself any differently than he had for dinner.

His shirt seemed dazzlingly white against the darkness of the shrubs.

Vilma felt a little throb of anxiety as she looked at him.

"You are ready, *Monsieur*?" the Referee asked the Marquis.

"I am ready!" the Marquis replied quietly.

He walked behind the Referee as he spoke, and taking Vilma's hand from her lap, raised it to his lips.

"I love you!" he said quietly.

She tried not to tremble, and it was impossible for her to speak.

For a moment they just looked into each other's eyes.

Then the Marquis moved away to stand in front of the Referee.

The *Comte* joined him.

At the same time, his two seconds, who were both young men, crossed to the opposite side of the Bowling-Green.

The two duellists stood in front of the Referee as he said to them in his quiet voice:

"You will stand back-to-back until I give the order to proceed. You will then walk pace by pace in opposite directions until, on the count of ten, you may turn and fire at each other."

He paused before he added:

"You will aim not higher than the shoulder of your opponent."

The two men took position back-to-back.

The Marquis was a head taller than the *Comte,* and his whole body looked athletic and lissom.

The Referee gave the word and they began to move.

It was then that Vilma, as if she could not remain seated, rose to her feet.

"One—two—three—" the Referee began as she watched the Marquis.

It then occurred to her, almost as if a voice were telling her to do so, that she should watch the *Comte.*

He looked extremely menacing with his black shirt and a black silk handkerchief round his neck.

"Five—six—seven—" the Referee was intoning.

The *Comte* and the Marquis had reached almost opposite ends of the Bowling-Green.

"Nine—!" the Referee called.

As he said the word, Vilma saw the *Comte* turn.

Even as he did so, she screamed.

Her cry rang out in the silence so that instinctively the Marquis turned round.

In the split second that he did so, he saw that the *Comte* was already facing him and he fired.

The *Comte*'s pistol exploded at what seemed to be exactly the same moment.

The Marquis had moved slightly to one side in turning at Vilma's cry.

The *Comte*'s bullet had obviously been intended to hit him in the back.

Instead it grazed his upper arm, tearing through the white silk of his shirt.

It was then that Vilma began to run towards him.

She reached him as he clasped his left hand over the wound.

Blood was already staining the whiteness of his shirt.

"That was disgraceful!" the Referee commented loudly.

"The man is a damned cheat!" Peter Hampton exclaimed furiously as he reached the Marquis. "He turned on the count of nine!"

"I know," the Marquis replied, "but Vilma's voice saved me."

Barker the valet was not talking.

He produced a bandage from his pocket with a swab of cotton-wool and was already tending to his Master.

"You'd better sit down, M'Lord," he said.

"I am all right," the Marquis answered. "It is only a scratch, thank God!"

As he spoke, he looked towards the other end of the Bowling-Green.

Without his saying anything, both Vilma and Peter Hampton followed the direction of his eyes.

They saw then that the *Comte* was lying on the ground.

His two seconds were bending over him, and Peter Hampton said:

"You must have hit him, Vernon."

"I hope so," the Marquis answered. "The man is a cheat, which I have heard before, but I never believed he could be so blatant about it."

"You may have hit him in the chest," Peter Hampton said. "I will go and find out."

As he hurried away, Vilma saw that the Marquis was swaying a little.

There was a wooden seat half-concealed amongst the bushes.

It was doubtless used by those who played Bowls.

"Come and sit down," she said. "Even a small wound can be a shock."

"That's quite right, Miss," the valet said, "an' 'Is Lordship's going to lose quite a lot o' blood."

It was already seeping through the cotton-wool and the bandage.

As if he did feel slightly weak, the Marquis allowed Vilma to draw him towards the seat.

He sat down, while the valet produced another bandage to cover the one that was already blood-stained.

Vilma did not speak, she only held the Marquis's hand.

He was looking towards the end of the Bowling-Green, where Peter was standing.

It was some minutes before he returned, picking up the Marquis's coat on his way back to them.

The Marquis looked up at him enquiringly.

"You hit him low in the shoulder," Peter explained, "and he is in a bad state. They are going to carry him to the house and send for a Doctor."

The Marquis did not reply. He merely nodded.

"If you ask me," Peter went on, "he deliberately did not arrange for a Doctor to be here so that if he had shot you in the back, as he intended to do, you would doubtless have died."

"I think I should go home, and you had better get me a Doctor," the Marquis said, "in case I need some stitches in this wound."

Vilma knew he was talking bravely.

At the same time, he was looking very pale.

He was obviously suffering from shock, which was just beginning to take effect.

He did not ask for any help.

She knew, however, as they walked back towards the carriage, that it was only with an effort that the Marquis held himself steady.

They got into the carriage, and Peter spoke to the coachman.

"I have instructed the driver to stop at the British Embassy," he explained. "I know the Doctor who looks after the Ambassador will come to you at once."

"I hope he will keep his mouth shut about all this," the Marquis said. "I do not want Miss Crawshaw to be involved."

"No, of course not," Peter agreed, "and I promise that you can trust him."

It did not take them long to reach the Ritz.

By that time the Marquis was definitely pale and unsteady on his feet.

His valet insisted that he should take his arm, hiding his blood-stained arm by putting his coat over his shoulders.

Then they moved as quickly as they could towards the stairs.

"Keep the carriage, Peter," the Marquis said before he went in through the door, "and take Miss Crawshaw home."

Vilma said nothing.

She had been afraid they might drop her off first and she would not know the outcome of the Doctor's visit.

When they reached the Marquis's Suite, Vilma waited in the Sitting-Room while his valet undressed him and got him into bed.

She could not keep still, but walked up and down.

She was praying desperately that he would not suffer too much.

She was aware that such a wound could turn septic and cause the victim to run a high temperature.

Before the valet could come and tell her that the Marquis was in bed, Peter Hampton appeared.

He had brought the Doctor up with him.

He was an elderly man who looked, Vilma thought, very competent.

Peter Hampton introduced them before the Doctor went into the Marquis's bedroom.

It seemed to Vilma as if several hours passed before Peter emerged, saying:

"It is all right. The wound is not as bad as we feared, but Vernon has lost a lot of blood and he will feel weak for a day or two."

Vilma gave a sigh of relief.

"I am sure that what he needs is quiet," she said, "so perhaps you would be kind enough to take me home."

"That is just what I was going to suggest," Peter replied. "Would you like first to say good-night to Vernon?"

It was what Vilma wanted more than anything else.

She realised, however, that the Doctor who had come from the Embassy might be shocked at her going into a man's bedroom.

"If you intend to come back afterwards," she said, "you can give him my good wishes for a speedy recovery."

Peter Hampton smiled at her.

"Of course I will do that," he said, "and I am sure that within forty-eight hours Vernon will be his old self again."

He opened the door of the Suite.

Vilma looked towards the closed door of the bedroom.

"Good-bye, my love," she whispered in her heart.

chapter seven

WHEN Vilma reached the house, she went straight to her bedroom, where Marie was waiting for her.

She asked no questions and Vilma did not speak until the *femme de Chambre* said good-night.

"*Bonsoir*, Marie," Vilma replied.

As the door shut, she lay back against her pillows.

She was trying to understand what had happened.

Yet she knew, that as far as she was concerned, it was the end of the world.

The shock of the Marquis saying he could not marry her because, apart from the fact that he was committed to Princess Helgie, her blood in any case was not good enough, swept over her like a tidal wave.

How was it possible that he did not realise that, fathered as she was, she could not be the daughter of even a superior craftsman.

She thought of how she had saved him from being killed by the *Comte*.

At least, she thought, she had played her part convincingly in what had begun as a game.

But the game for her had become a fairy-story.

Now that too had come to an end.

Slowly the tears began to fall from her eyes and run down her cheeks.

Gradually the lump, which had felt so heavy in her heart and made her feel numb to everything that was happening, went.

It was then she knew that she had lost him.

The love that had come to her like a light from Heaven was only part of a dream.

"I love . . . him! I love . . . him!" she sobbed.

Her life would never be the same again.

It had been an enchantment to be with the Marquis every day, to talk to him alone at luncheon and dinner and to drive with him in the *Bois*, to see Paris with him by night.

To him it had just been an ordinary, everyday episode.

But to her it had been like being in Paradise with the Angels singing.

It was what she had expected love would be like.

But the love she bore for the Marquis was not the same as the love he had for her.

Thinking back over their conversations, she realised he had put her in the same category as "La Belle Otero," the woman whose name her Father had forbidden her to mention.

The *Comte* had thought of her in the same way.

The full horror of the duel between the two men fighting for possession of her struck her for the first time.

"How could I have . . . allowed it to . . . happen?"

she asked. "How could I have . . . actually gone to watch it take place?"

In her innocence and purity, when they had said they were fighting for her, she had not understood what they intended.

The Marquis, however, now had made it abundantly clear.

He wanted her as his mistress, while he was married to another woman.

As she cried, and went on crying, Vilma felt as if she had sunk into a slough of despair.

She was no longer clean and decent, but dirty and degraded by the whole affair.

"It is all my own fault," she sobbed. "I should have told the Marquis from . . . the moment he . . . saved me from the *Comte* that I was . . . not an Electrician."

She remembered her Nanny saying that one lie leads to another.

She had allowed him to believe that she was helping her Father install the electricity in the *Vicomte*'s house.

She cried until she was exhausted.

Only when the sun was rising over the horizon did she fall asleep.

She had no idea that Marie peeped into her room and went away without waking her.

* * *

When finally Vilma stirred, she realised that the curtains were being drawn back from the windows.

The sunshine was pouring in.

"I am sorry to wake you, *M'mselle,* when you're so tired," Marie said, "but *M'sieur* Blanc wants to have a word with you about your Father before he leaves."

Vilma sat up in bed.

"What time is it?" she asked.

"It's half-past ten, *M'mselle*."

"Good gracious! Can it be so late?" Vilma exclaimed.

She got out of bed.

Marie fetched her *negligée*, which was more elaborate than her dressing-gown.

Because he was more or less a Doctor, Vilma thought it would not matter if she saw him without being fully dressed.

As she tied back her long hair with a bow of satin ribbon, she asked:

"Where is *Monsieur* Blanc?"

"In the *Boudoir, M'mselle*," Marie replied.

The *Boudoir* was the room leading from her Father's bedroom.

Vilma hurried along the passage towards it.

Pierre Blanc was standing looking out of the window as she entered.

"Bonjour, Monsieur," she said. "I must apologise, but I was late to bed last night and in consequence have over-slept."

"It is something which often happens in Paris, *Mademoiselle*," Pierre Blanc replied. "I wanted to speak to you about *Monsieur* your Father, as I shall not need to come here again."

Vilma looked at him in surprise.

"Does that mean that Papa is already cured?"

She thought it was hardly possible, but Pierre Blanc nodded.

"The bones of his back are now reset," he said, "and

he will be no longer troubled if he takes things very carefully for at least a month."

"It is wonderful that you have healed him," Vilma said, "and we are extremely grateful to you."

"Your Father's case was not as difficult as some I have handled," Pierre Blanc said. "His fall displaced several bones, but fortunately they were not damaged."

"And he really is all right?" Vilma asked as if she could not quite believe it.

"As I have said, he must be careful," Pierre Blanc replied, "and I have warned him—no riding for at least six weeks!"

"It is going to be difficult to keep him off a horse until then," Vilma remarked.

"I think your Father is sensible enough to realise that he does not want a return of the excruciating pain he was suffering when he came here," Pierre Blanc said.

"Will he not feel as tired as he did while you have been treating him?" Vilma asked.

Pierre Blanc smiled.

"The tiredness, or rather the desire for sleep, was due in some part to the herbs I gave him."

Vilma made a little exclamation, and he went on:

"It was essential that he should remain as still as possible, and it is difficult to keep an active man from moving about and making his condition worse."

"I understand," Vilma replied.

"Try to keep your Father as quiet as you can and, as I have said, away from the stables for six weeks."

"I will try, I promise you I will try," Vilma replied, "and thank you very much indeed. I am more grateful to you than I can possibly say."

They shook hands, and the Frenchman hurried away, presumably to see other patients who were waiting for him.

As soon as he had gone, Vilma went to her Father's bedroom.

He was sitting up in bed looking almost himself and reading the newspapers.

"Good-morning, Vilma!" the Earl said heartily. "I expect you have heard the good news."

"I have indeed, Papa," Vilma said as she kissed him. "I am so glad, and so very, very grateful to *Monsieur* Blanc."

"The man is exceedingly clever, and the reports I had of him were not exaggerated," the Earl said.

He put down the newspaper.

"Now we can go back to England, but I am afraid you will have missed many of the Balls on my account."

"That does not matter, Papa," Vilma said.

"It matters very much in your first Season," the Earl replied as if he wanted to be argumentative. "And your *Beaux* will be waiting for you."

Vilma felt like saying that the only *Beau* she wanted was in Paris, but he was inaccessible.

It passed through her mind that the best thing she could do now would be to return as soon as possible to London with her Father.

She could not bear to have to confess to the Marquis that she had deceived him.

Worse than that would be to listen to his apology for thinking her to be in an inferior social class to his own.

Aloud she said:

"That is what we will do, Papa. We will go back

to England tomorrow, and as you have to be very careful of yourself, we must try to book a private Drawing-Room on the train."

There was silence for a moment. Then the Earl said:

"That is not a bad idea. See if you can arrange to have one attached to the express."

"I will," Vilma promised.

She bent and kissed her Father's cheek and said:

"It will be lovely to be back in England again and . . . perhaps forget what has happened in Paris."

She was speaking almost to herself, but the Earl replied:

"I am exceedingly glad I came. I do not believe there is a man in England who could do for me what Pierre Blanc has done."

Vilma went back to her own room and dressed quickly.

She then sent for the Butler, who told her that it was he who always organised the *Vicomte*'s travelling arrangements.

He promised he would go at once to the *Gare du Nord*.

If it was possible, he would obtain a private Drawing-Room on the express to Calais.

Vilma thanked him and said they would like to leave the next day.

The man looked worried.

"That might be difficult, *M'mselle*. They like more than a day's notice for a Drawing-Room, which is not always available."

"Then try to arrange it for as soon as possible," Vilma begged.

She had just given these instructions when Peter Hampton was announced.

"Good-morning, Miss Crawshaw!" he said. "Vernon asked me to bring you up-to-date news of his condition which, on the whole, is satisfactory."

Vilma drew in her breath.

"I am so glad," she said. "I have been very worried."

"The Doctor called first thing this morning," Peter Hampton went on, "and although the wound is inflamed, Vernon's temperature has not risen very high and should go down within the next twenty-four hours."

"He is . . . not in pain?" Vilma asked quickly.

"A wound like that is always unpleasant," Peter Hampton replied, "but the Doctor has given him something to help him sleep, and I am sure he will feel better tomorrow."

"I suppose there is nothing more we can do for him?" Vilma asked vaguely.

"I assure you he has everything he wants," Peter Hampton answered. "César Ritz has been most concerned about his condition and has sent him fruit and flowers and Heaven knows what else!"

"I find him a very kind man," Vilma said.

Peter Hampton looked round the room.

"Vernon tells me you are an expert in electricity," he said. "Are you responsible for the lighting in this house?"

There was a little pause before Vilma said:

"No, I am not, and I am afraid the Marquis overestimates my capabilities."

"Well, I thought it was very brave of you to come to the duel last night," Peter remarked, "and there is no doubt that you saved Vernon from being badly injured, if not killed."

"How could anyone behave so wickedly?" Vilma asked. "The *Comte* should not be allowed to go free to treat other men in the same manner."

"Do not worry about that," Peter replied. "I intend to make certain that no-one will ever fight a duel with him in the future."

"How can you do that?" Vilma asked.

"I am going to tell the British Ambassador about his disgraceful behaviour, and I am quite certain the Referee, who is a distinguished man, will talk to a number of French aristocrats who are very particular about protocol and that sort of thing."

"And so they ought to be!" Vilma said indignantly.

"I agree with you," Peter Hampton said, "and if the *Comte* finds himself ostracised by all those of importance in French Society, he will never again have the opportunity of behaving so abominably."

He glanced at the clock and exclaimed:

"If I am to catch the Ambassador before luncheon, I must dash!"

"Thank you for coming," Vilma said, "and please tell the Marquis I hope he will soon be better."

"I will give him your message," Peter said.

Vilma walked with him to the front-door.

She was aware that he was looking at her with undisguised admiration.

He held her hand for longer than was necessary as he said:

"Good-bye, Miss Crawshaw. I trust I may call again tomorrow to bring you further reports on the condition of our invalid."

"I hope you will do that," Vilma replied, "and thank you again for coming to see me this morning."

She watched him drive away, then went back into the Drawing-Room.

She was thinking that if she and her Father were going home tomorrow, she should write to the Marquis.

She must make it clear that he would not be able to get in touch with her.

"It is finished . . . finished!" she told herself.

Sitting down at the *Secrétaire* by the window, she picked up a pen.

* * *

Vilma had written very little, when she was told that luncheon was being served upstairs.

Her Father wanted her to eat with him.

She looked at what she had written.

Then she tore it up into small pieces, before she threw it into the waste-paper basket.

When she got upstairs, it was to find that her Father was out of bed.

He was wearing a dressing-gown and had moved into the *Boudoir*.

A table for two had been laid in the centre of it.

When he saw Vilma, the Earl exclaimed:

"You see, my dear, I am on my feet, but Herbert refuses to let me dress, and has commanded that I am to return to bed after the wild dissipation of having luncheon with you!"

Vilma laughed.

"You know we all have to obey Herbert," she said, "and of course he is right, Papa. Pierre Blanc has been giving me strict instructions as to how you are to behave when you get back to England."

"There is nothing worse than being an invalid and having nagging women and domineering man-servants and Doctors ordering one about!" the Earl grumbled.

He was, however, Vilma knew, delighted to be on his feet.

They drank a little champagne to celebrate the occasion.

"I have asked the Butler to book us a Drawing-Room," Vilma told him, "but he says it may be difficult to obtain one at such short notice for tomorrow."

"I expect he will manage it if we pay enough," the Earl said cynically.

He was right.

When the Butler returned, he told Vilma that he had, only with the greatest difficulty and a generous amount of bribery, obtained a Drawing-Room.

But it was for the evening express which travelled to Calais by night.

Vilma thought perhaps it would be better for her Father to sleep in the train.

He would at least be fresh to endure the rest of the journey, which might involve a rough passage across the Channel.

After that, there would be some hours in the train from Dover to Victoria.

Vilma thanked the Butler for all the trouble he had taken.

She was certain her Father would tip him handsomely before they left.

Then she went up to her bedroom to start writing her letter all over again.

Finally she had written what she thought was both kind and frank.

She read it through slowly.

The fairy-story has come to an end.

It is difficult to thank you enough for your kindness to me while I have been in Paris.

I shall never forget the beauty of the Place de la Concorde. I shall remember, too, the Bois and the delightful dinner we had in the Grand Vefour.

Thank you for such memories, and I wish you every happiness in the future.

Vilma

She put it in an envelope and left it on the *Secrétaire*.

She thought she would give it to Peter Hampton when he called the following morning.

She decided she should buy a few presents for her friends in England, those who would have missed her at the Balls and dinner-parties which she had not attended.

She wanted a special present for her Aunt, who had presented her at Court.

When Vilma talked to her Father later in the afternoon, she suggested they should not go to their London house, but return to the country.

"What about your Balls and parties?" the Earl asked with a frown.

"I have no wish to go to them, Papa. I would much rather be with you, especially when you will find it tiresome not to be able to ride."

She saw the obstinate expression on his face and said quickly:

"You have to obey Pierre Blanc's orders. So we will

walk in the garden and fish in the lake, which we have not done for a long time."

She paused for a moment and then went on:

"I am sure there are many improvements you want to make on the Estate. Here is your opportunity to drive round and give instructions about them."

The Earl, who realised exactly what she was doing, put his hand on her shoulder.

"You are a good girl, Vilma," he said, "and having deprived you of the frivolities of the London Season, I promise you shall have the biggest and finest Ball anybody could have in the Autumn."

What he said made Vilma feel guilty.

The real reason why she did not wish to go back to London was that she had no wish to dance with young men in whom she had no interest.

She knew that every one of them would compare unfavourably with the Marquis.

She also feared that she might encounter him at one of the more important Balls.

That, she thought, was something to be avoided at all costs.

She would be much safer in the country.

There would be no chance of her running into him there by mistake.

She knew if she saw him again it would be an agony not to throw herself into his arms, to beg him to kiss her just once more.

"I doubt if he would want to once he knows who I am," she said to herself. "Anyway, he will have the Princess as his wife."

She might be very brave in the daylight, but when night came she buried her face in her pillow and wept.

* * *

As she expected, Peter Hampton called about noon.

"I have come to give you the latest news," he said.

"I do hope His Lordship is better," Vilma said primly.

"He did not have a very good night," Peter Hampton told her. "His valet said he was restless and his wound is painful."

"So he is still in bed?" Vilma asked.

"Of course!" Peter Hampton replied. "The Doctor has forbidden him to get up for at least another day or two."

That was what Vilma wanted to hear.

She talked to Peter Hampton for a little while.

Then she gave him the letter that was waiting on the *Secrétaire*.

Before he left, he asked Vilma to dine with him, but she refused.

"It is very kind of you," she answered, "but my Father is better and he will want me to be with him."

"I will ask you again tomorrow," Peter Hampton said, "if Vernon is still *hors de combat*."

Vilma knew he would not have dreamt of asking her to dine with him alone if he had known who she really was.

He, in his turn, had assumed that she was merely an Electrician's daughter.

Peter Hampton drove away.

Vilma knew that when he returned tomorrow she and her Father would have left the *Vicomte*'s house.

On Herbert's instructions, the Earl was to stay in bed until the very last moment.

Vilma calculated they would not leave for the *Gare du Nord* until about seven o'clock.

After luncheon she tried to read a book in order to pass the time.

But the pages swam in front of her eyes, and she had not absorbed a single word.

She gave a sigh and walked to the open window.

There was a small garden at the back of the house.

It did not compare with the *Comte*'s garden in which the duel had been fought.

Peter Hampton had told her that the *Comte* was very ill indeed.

She could not help being pleased about that.

She knew that if he was suffering, it was no less than what he had intended to inflict upon the Marquis.

Even to think of the Marquis made it difficult to keep the tears from flooding into her eyes.

She was seeing the garden through a haze when she heard the door open behind her.

"Monsieur le Marquis of Lynworth to see you, *M'mselle*!" she heard a servant say.

She turned round.

Incredible though it seemed, the Marquis was standing there.

His arm was in a sling and he was looking very pale.

Otherwise, he was as handsome and as irresistible as ever.

The servant shut the door.

For a moment neither of them moved.

They just stood looking at each other.

Vilma felt as if the whole room was filled with a dazzling light.

Then slowly the Marquis walked towards her.

As he reached her, she said in a little voice that did not sound like her own:

"W-why . . . are you . . . here? I . . . I thought the . . . Doctor said . . . that you were . . . not to . . . get up."

"I could not stay in bed," the Marquis said in a deep voice, "because when I received your letter I knew that you were going away."

"H-how do you know . . . that?" Vilma asked.

"I think we've always known what the other is thinking," the Marquis said, "without words."

She glanced up at him, afraid, or perhaps shy, of meeting his eyes.

Then he said quietly:

"I have come, my Darling, to ask you if you will do me the honour of becoming my wife."

For a moment Vilma could not move or breathe.

Then, as she looked at him in bewilderment, he said:

"Forgive me! How can I have been such a fool as not to realise that nothing in life matters to me except you? I love you, I want you! Already you belong to me, as I belong to you!"

"But . . . but . . ." Vilma began.

The Marquis put his arm around her.

"There are no 'buts,' " he said. "We are going to be married, whatever the world may say."

Then his lips were on hers, and she felt her whole body melt into his.

She knew that, as he had said, they were part of each other and completely inseparable.

When at last the Marquis raised his head she said:

"It . . . it . . . was wrong of you to . . . come here . . . when you have . . . been . . . told to . . . stay in . . . b-bed."

"How could I do that when I might have lost you?" the Marquis asked. "And you have not yet told me, my Darling, how soon you will marry me."

Vilma put her head against his shoulder.

"I . . . love . . . you!" she said.

"That is the only thing that matters," the Marquis replied.

She wanted to say more but turned her face up to his and he was kissing her again.

His arm was as strong as steel as he drew her closer and closer.

To Vilma it was as if the Angels were singing.

The room was illuminated with a light which could only have come from Heaven.

They heard the door open.

Vilma quickly moved away from the Marquis, wondering who had interrupted them.

When she looked round she saw that a man had come into the room whom she had never seen before.

He was middle-aged, good-looking, and had an unmistakable air of importance.

He was walking towards her, when he saw the Marquis and gave an exclamation.

"Good Heavens! Lynworth!" he said. "I did not expect to find you here! I heard when I arrived an hour ago that you had been wounded in a duel."

"How could you have heard that?" the Marquis asked.

"I was told by your Referee, who is a relation of mine," the stranger replied. "It is unlike you to let your opponent get the better of you!"

He then turned to Vilma.

"You must be my guest," he said. "I can only apologise that I was not here to greet you and your Father when you arrived."

Vilma had been listening as if bemused.

Now she realised that this must be the *Vicomte* and that he had arrived home unexpectedly.

With an effort she managed to say:

"M-my Father is . . . much better. We are extremely grateful to you for allowing us to stay here while he was undergoing . . . his treatment."

"I knew Blanc would not fail," the *Vicomte* said. "But my servants tell me that you are leaving tonight."

"Papa is . . . eager to go back to . . . England," Vilma explained.

"I suppose he is missing his horses." The *Vicomte* smiled.

He turned again to look at the Marquis, saying:

"I am sure you and Cuttesdale have found a great deal in common when it comes to horses. I was delighted to hear that you won the Derby, and of course the Earl won the Two-Thousand Guinea Stakes."

Vilma saw the astonishment on the Marquis's face.

But before he could say anything, the *Vicomte* said to her:

"I will just go upstairs, Lady Vilma, and tell your Father I am here. Wait for me, Lynworth, and we will have a glass of champagne. I feel you deserve it after being in the wars!"

He laughed at his own joke, as he went from the room.

Only when the door had closed behind him did the Marquis ask:

"What was he talking about? I do not understand."

"I will . . . explain," Vilma replied. "My . . . my

Father came to Paris for treatment because he had an . . . accident out riding."

She hesitated, then continued when he remained silent:

"He did not want . . . anybody to know that he had had a fall which had injured his spine. We therefore travelled under assumed names—or at least Crawshaw is one of . . . Papa's . . . lesser titles."

She was aware that she was stammering the words.

The Marquis was staring at her in surprise, and also as if he were annoyed.

She was not mistaken.

"How can you have deceived me?" he asked. "Why did you not tell me who you were?"

Vilma lowered her eyes, and without looking at him said:

"Papa was . . . insistent that he should not meet any of his . . . friends here . . . and be laughed at for so ignominiously falling from his horse. When you assumed that he was an . . . Electrician . . . and . . . I was helping him . . . I did not dare . . . contradict you."

"Then what were you doing up that ladder in the *Comte*'s bedroom?" the Marquis asked.

"One of the new chandeliers had been smashed on delivery to the Hotel, and *Monsieur* Ritz came here to ask if he could borrow one of the *Vicomte*'s, which he had used as a model."

She glanced up at the Marquis as he looked at her angrily.

"He then invited me to go back with him so that I could . . . see the Hotel for myself. Then . . . while the Electrician went off to get some . . . bulbs, I cleaned off some dirty marks, knowing it would . . . annoy *Monsieur* Ritz to see them."

She glanced at the Marquis from under her eyelashes.

He was still looking angry, and she went on quickly:

"*Monsieur* Ritz went off to attend to something in the Hotel, and when I was alone . . . the *Comte* came into the bedroom and assumed, as you did, that I was . . . working there."

"You mean," the Marquis said, "that everything that happened was just because you were trying to help César Ritz."

"It seems very . . . stupid when you . . . put it like . . . that," Vilma murmured, "but he was so . . . proud of all his . . . rooms."

The Marquis did not say anything, and after a moment she begged.

"Please . . . forgive me . . . I wanted to tell you . . . then . . . when you suggested . . ."

She could not say any more, and the Marquis finished the sentence for her:

"When I thought you were the daughter of an Electrician and asked you to become my mistress! Surely you might have told me then?"

Vilma moved to stand at the window with her back to him.

"I know that is what I . . . could have done," she said, "but . . . if I had told you . . . it would have seemed as if I were . . . forcing myself on you."

"Instead of which you were prepared to leave me and go away and forget me," the Marquis protested.

"I should . . . never have . . . forgotten you," Vilma said.

There was silence.

Then he said:

"I know now that I should have realised very quickly that you simply could not be just an Electrician's daughter. Can you ever forgive me for being so stupid? And can you, please, give me an answer to the question I came here to ask you?"

Vilma felt her heart leap.

"Do you . . . want . . . an answer?" she asked.

The Marquis put out his arm and turned her round.

"You answered me in fact when you kissed me," he said, "and you are going to be my wife. Only now it is going to be very much easier than I thought it would be."

"And you really . . . love me enough to . . . brave your family and everybody else who would have been horrified at your marrying the daughter of an . . . Electrician?"

"Of course I do!" the Marquis declared. "I am afraid there are still pitfalls ahead. But I know, my Precious, that I cannot live without you. Anyway, my life became your responsibility after the duel."

Vilma put her head on his shoulder.

"I think it was . . . God who . . . told me that I must . . . watch the *Comte* and . . . not you. I had a feeling he was going to do something wicked, but I never thought it would be as shocking as shooting to . . . kill you when you had your . . . back to him!"

"We need not worry about him any more," the Marquis said. "Peter is dealing with him from the British point of view, and he tells me that our Referee will see that he is ostracised by every decent Frenchman."

He pulled Vilma a little closer before he said:

"Now we can talk about ourselves, and as I am marrying somebody who is not only very beautiful but also very important, there is no reason why either of us should be afraid of anything."

"What about the . . . Princess?" Vilma asked.

The Marquis shrugged his shoulders.

"I have not asked her to be my wife, and if I am engaged to be married when she arrives in England, she will just have to look elsewhere for a husband."

"There will not be any . . . trouble about your not . . . asking her to be your wife?"

"If there is, it is doubtful if anybody will complain to me personally," the Marquis said, "and when they see you, my precious one, they will know exactly why I prefer you to a Princess."

He was laughing as he said the last words.

Then he was kissing Vilma as he had kissed her before, but even more insistently, more demandingly.

It was as if he were determined that there should be no opposition to their being married.

* * *

The *Vicomte* came downstairs to say to Vilma:

"Your Father insists that we all go to talk to him in the *Boudoir*. He says he is very eager to see you, Lynworth, and I have the feeling it is because he wants to talk about your horses."

"I have something of much greater importance to talk about to him!" the Marquis said.

The *Vicomte* looked from one to the other and said:

"I think I can guess what it is—or would it be indiscreet?"

"Vilma is going to marry me," the Marquis said proudly, "and we have no wish to waste a lot of time talking about it."

The *Vicomte* put his hand on the Marquis's shoulder.

"Congratulations!" he said. "And now that I have seen Lady Vilma, I can understand why you are in a hurry!"

They all went upstairs and Vilma, holding on to the Marquis's hand, knew she had stepped back into her fairy-story.

It had not come to an end.

In fact, when she saw the expression in the Marquis's eyes, she knew it was just beginning.

As if the *Vicomte* felt he must get into the act, when he opened the door to the *Boudoir,* where the Earl was seated in a comfortable armchair, he simultaneously announced:

"Here we are, and your daughter and Lynworth have something very important to tell you."

Vilma released the Marquis's hand and ran to her Father's side.

"Do not be angry, Papa," she begged, "but I met the Marquis while you were having your treatment and we are very, very happy."

"What are you saying? What is all this about?" the Earl asked.

The Marquis went up to his chair.

"Your daughter, My Lord, has promised to marry me," he said, "and I hope you will give us your blessing."

"You certainly have that," the Earl replied. "I always hoped she would have the good sense to marry somebody of whom I approve, and how can I do anything else when your horses keep beating mine to the post!"

The Marquis laughed.

"If you will allow me to marry Vilma," he said, "I think we can arrange not to compete with each other, but only against every other stable in the country."

"I will certainly agree to that," the Earl replied, his eyes twinkling.

The two older men toasted the young couple with champagne and wished them every happiness.

Vilma said later:

"I think, Papa, that Vernon should return to the Ritz and go back to bed. He was told by his Doctor that he was not to get up for at least two days, and he came here in defiance of those orders."

"There is no reason to go back to the Ritz," the *Vicomte* said before the Earl could reply. "Stay here, Lynworth, then we can all dine together, even if you and the Earl are unable to dress up."

"My Father and I are supposed to be leaving tomorrow," Vilma interposed.

"Nonsense!" the *Vicomte* said before the Earl could speak. "I cannot have my party going away so soon. I want to talk to your Father about race-horses, and, of course, your fiancé can contribute his opinions."

He paused before he continued. Looking at the Earl, he said:

"Stay with me for at least another two days. I really need you."

The Earl spread out his hands.

"How can I refuse when you have been so kind to me already?"

"I will tell the Butler to cancel the Drawing-Room on the train," Vilma said, "but I do think Vernon should lie down. He still has a temperature."

The *Vicomte* rose to his feet.

"You had better do as you are told, Lynworth," he said, "and there are plenty of bedrooms for you to choose from. I will send to the Ritz for your luggage."

He walked from the room as he spoke, and Vilma put her hand on the Marquis's arm.

"Do you want us to stay?" she asked.

"Do you think I would let you go to London without me?" the Marquis replied. "Wherever you go, I am coming too."

"There are quite a number of things I want to discuss with the *Vicomte,*" the Earl said, "so it will suit me to stay here for another two days."

He got up as he spoke, and walked out of the *Boudoir* towards his bedroom.

He had almost reached the door when he said, following his train of thought:

"Oh, by the way, I see in *Le Jour* that the Grand Duke of Whitenburg has just died of a heart-attack. You will remember, Lynworth, his horse won the *Grand Prix* last year."

He was not aware as he left the room that the Marquis was staring after him as if he could hardly believe what he had heard.

As he put his arm round Vilma, he knew that Fate, or perhaps her prayers, had brought him unbelievable good luck.

He could hardly credit it was true.

If the Grand Duke had died, then there would be no thought of Princess Helgie coming to England.

Nor could there be any possibility, while she was in mourning, of her marriage being even considered for at least a year.

He was completely free from any commitment his Mother might have made.

He knew as he pulled Vilma to him that he was the most fortunate man in the whole world.

"I love you, my Darling," he said. "I love you so

much that I know I will grudge every moment we are not together. Persuade your Father that we must be married immediately! In fact, as soon as we set foot on English soil."

Vilma lifted her lips up to his.

"I want to be married," she said, "but . . . I think we must wait until your shoulder has healed . . . or too many people will ask awkward questions as to why it is in a sling."

"The only question I am going to answer," the Marquis said, "is the one asking 'Why do I love you?' The answer to that is that you are the most perfect person in the world!"

"Please . . . go on thinking . . . that," Vilma said, "and, as far as I am concerned . . . no other man exists . . . except you."

As the Marquis kissed her, she knew it was true.

She loved him with every breath she drew and, as he had said, they were completely one person.

She knew as his kisses grew more passionate, more demanding, that though everyone sought love many failed to find it.

Theirs was a love that was invincible, inescapable, theirs for eternity.

Her whole body was singing with the wonder of the Marquis's kisses.

She knew that the ecstasy that seeped through her like the sunshine was moving in him.

"My Darling, my sweet! The woman I have been seeking all my life!" the Marquis murmured.

Then there was only the dazzling light of Love which came from God.

It would protect, guide, and inspire them for as long as they lived.

ABOUT THE AUTHOR

Barbara Cartland, the world's most famous romantic novelist, who is also an historian, playwright, lecturer, political speaker and television personality, has now written over 583 books and sold over six hundred and twenty million copies all over the world.

She had also had many historical works published and has written four autobiographies as well as the biographies of her mother and that of her brother, Ronald Cartland, who was the first Member of Parliament to be killed in the last war. This book had a preface by Sir Winston Churchill and has just been republished with an introduction by Sir Arthur Bryant.

Love at the Helm, a novel written with the help and inspiration of the late Earl Mountbatten of Burma, Great Uncle of His Royal Highness, The Prince of Wales, is being sold for the Mountbatten Memorial Trust.

She has broken the world record for the last nineteen

years by writing an average of twenty-three books a year. In the *Guinness Book of World Records* she is listed as the world's top-selling author.

Miss Cartland in 1987 sang an Album of Love Songs with the Royal Philharmonic Orchestra.

In private life Barbara Cartland, who is a Dame of the Order of St. John of Jerusalem, Chairman of the St. John Council in Hertfordshire and Deputy President of the St. John Ambulance Brigade, has fought for better conditions and salaries for Mid-wives and Nurses.

She championed the cause for the Elderly in 1956 invoking a Government Enquiry into the "Housing Condition of Old People."

In 1962 she had the Law of England changed so that Local Authorities had to provide camps for their own Gypsies. This has meant that since then thousands and thousands of Gypsy children have been able to go to School, which they had never been able to do in the past, as their caravans were moved every twenty-four hours by the Police.

There are now fourteen camps in Hertfordshire and Barbara Cartland has her own Romany Gypsy Camp called Barbaraville by the Gypsies.

Her designs "Decorating with Love" are being sold all over the U.S.A. and the National Home Fashions League made her, in 1981, "Woman of Achievement."

She is unique in that she was one and two in the Dalton list of Best Sellers, and one week had four books in the top twenty.

Barbara Cartland's book *Getting Older, Growing Younger* has been published in Great Britain and the U.S.A. and her fifth cookery book, *The Romance of Food,* is now being used by the House of Commons.

In 1984 she received at Kennedy Airport America's Bishop Wright Air Industry Award for her contribution to the development of aviation. In 1931 she and two R.A.F. Officers thought of, and carried, the first aeroplane-towed glider airmail.

During the War she was Chief Lady Welfare Officer in Bedfordshire, looking after 20,000 Servicemen and -women. She thought of having a pool of Wedding Dresses at the War Office so a Service Bride could hire a gown for the day.

She bought 1,000 gowns without coupons for the A.T.S., the W.A.A.F.'s and the W.R.E.N.S. In 1945 Barbara Cartland received the Certificate of Merit from Eastern Command.

In 1964 Barbara Cartland founded the National Association for Health of which she is the President, as a front for all the Health Stores and for any product made as alternative medicine.

This is now a £65 million turnover a year, with one-third going in export.

In January 1968 she received *La Médeille de Vermeil de la Ville de Paris*. This is the highest award to be given in France by the City of Paris. She has sold 25 million books in France.

Barbara Cartland was received with great enthusiasm by her fans, who feted her at a reception in the City, and she received the gift of an embossed plate from the Government.

In March 1988 Barbara Cartland was asked by the Indian Government to open their Health Resort outside Delhi. This is almost the largest Health Resort in the world.

Barbara Cartland was made a Dame of the Order of the British Empire in the 1991 New Year's Honours

List by Her Majesty, The Queen, for her contribution to Literature and also for her years of work for the community.

Dame Barbara has now written the greatest number of books by a British author, passing the 564 books written by John Creasey.

AWARDS

1945 Received Certificate of Merit, Eastern Command, for being Welfare Officer to 5,000 troops in Bedfordshire.

1953 Made a Commander of the Order of St. John of Jerusalem. Invested by H.R.H. The Duke of Gloucester at Buckingham Palace.

1972 Invested as Dame of Grace of the Order of St. John in London by The Lord Prior, Lord Cacia.

1981 Received "Achiever of the Year" from the National Home Furnishing Association in Colorado Springs, U.S.A., for her designs for wallpaper and fabrics.

1984 Received Bishop Wright Air Industry Award at Kennedy Airport, for inventing the aeroplane-towed glider.

1988 Received from Monsieur Chirac, The Prime Minister, The Gold Medal of the City of Paris, at the Hotel de la Ville, Paris, for selling 25 million books and giving a lot of employment.

1991 Invested as Dame of the Order of The British Empire, by H.M. The Queen at Buckingham Palace for her contribution to Literature.